ALASKA GEOGR

Volume 19, Number 1

SKAGWAY: A Legacy of Gold

The Alaska Geographic Society

To teach many more to better know and more wisely use our natural resources

EDITOR
Penny Rennick

PRODUCTION DIRECTOR
Kathy Doogan

STAFF WRITER
L.J. Campbell

MARKETING MANAGER
Jan Westfall

CIRCULATION/DATABASE MANAGER
Kevin Kerns

MARKETING/OFFICE ASSISTANT
Tracy Reid

ALASKA GEOGRAPHIC® (ISSN 0361-1353) is published quarterly by The Alaska Geographic Society, 137 East 7th Avenue, Anchorage, AK 99501. Second-class postage paid at Anchorage, Alaska, and additional mailing offices. Printed in U.S.A. Copyright © 1992 by The Alaska Geographic Society. All rights reserved. Registered trademark: Alaska Geographic, ISSN 0361-1353; Key title Alaska Geographic.
POSTMASTER: Send address changes to
ALASKA GEOGRAPHIC®
P.O. Box 93370
Anchorage, Alaska 99509-3370

COVER: *Skagway, population 700, is tucked into a fold in the Coast Mountains along the Skagway River valley. The town fronts on Skagway Bay, a bulge in Taiya Inlet at the head of Lynn Canal. To the left is Nahku or Long Bay. The valley beyond Skagway leads to White Pass.* (Dedman's Photo Shop)

PREVIOUS PAGE: *Visitors flock to Skagway during summer, making it one of Alaska's most visited tourist destinations. This July 1991 scene shows Broadway Street, in the heart of the downtown historic district.* (Harry M. Walker)

FACING PAGE: *A diesel-powered White Pass and Yukon passenger train crosses a trestle bridge at Glacier Station, a flag stop at mile 14.* (Dedman's Photo Shop)

BOARD OF DIRECTORS
Robert A. Henning, *President Emeritus*,
Judge Thomas Stewart, Phyllis Henning, Jim Brooks,
Charles Herbert, Celia Hunter, Byron Mallott,
Dr. Glen Olds, Penny Rennick

NATIONAL ADVISORS
Gilbert Grosvenor, Bradford Washburn, Dr. John Reed

THE ALASKA GEOGRAPHIC SOCIETY is a non-profit organization exploring new frontiers of knowledge across the lands of the Polar Rim, putting the geography book back in the classroom, exploring new methods of teaching and learning—sharing in the excitement of discovery in man's wonderful new world north of 51°16′.
MEMBERS OF THE SOCIETY receive *ALASKA GEOGRAPHIC*®, a quality magazine that devotes each quarterly issue to monographic in-depth coverage of a northern geographic region or resource-oriented subject.
MEMBERSHIP DUES in The Alaska Geographic Society are $39 per year, $49 to non-U.S. addresses. ($31.20 of the $39 yearly dues is for a one-year subscription to *ALASKA GEOGRAPHIC*®.) Order from The Alaska Geographic Society, P.O. Box 93370, Anchorage, AK 99509-3370; phone (907) 258-2515, FAX (907) 278-6582.
MATERIALS SOUGHT: *ALASKA GEOGRAPHIC*® editors seek a wide variety of informative material on the lands north of 51°16′ on geographic subjects—anything to do with resources and their uses (with heavy emphasis on quality color photography)—from all the lands of the Polar Rim and the economically related North Pacific Rim. We cannot be responsible for unsolicited submissions. Submissions not accompanied by sufficient postage for return by certified mail will be returned by regular mail.
CHANGE OF ADDRESS: The post office does not automatically forward *ALASKA GEOGRAPHIC*® when you move. To ensure continuous service, please notify us six weeks before moving. Send your new address and zip code, and, if possible, your membership number or a mailing label from a recent copy of *ALASKA GEOGRAPHIC*® to: *ALASKA GEOGRAPHIC*®, P.O. Box 93370, Anchorage, AK 99509-3370.
MAILING LISTS: We occasionally make our members' names and addresses available to carefully screened publications and companies whose products and activities may be of interest to you. If you prefer not to receive such mailings, please advise us, and include your mailing label (or your name and address if label is not available).

ABOUT THIS ISSUE: Staff writer L.J. Campbell compiled the major chapters for this issue. We send a special thank you to Frank Norris, historian with the National Park Service. Frank wrote the article on Skagway's gardens and thoroughly reviewed the manuscript. Skagway resident Su Rappleye wrote the profiles on some of the town's more enduring citizens: Oscar Selmer, Barbara Dedman Kalen, Marian Katseek Kelm, Bob Rapuzzi and Paul Jones.
We appreciate the assistance of Jeff Brady, editor of *The Skagway News*; Stan Selmer, Skagway's mayor; Jerre O'Farrell Fuqua; Silas Dennis Sr.; Carl Mulvihill; Boyd Worley; Steve Hites; Barbara Kalen; the National Park Service staff in Skagway; Harry M. Walker; Rose Schreier, Alaska State Library, Juneau; Bruce Merrell, Loussac Library, Anchorage; Lt. Col. Lyman Woodman, retired USAF; and Tom Morgan, KAKM, Anchorage.

COLOR SEPARATIONS BY: Graphic Chromatics

PRINTED BY: Hart Press

PRICE TO NON-MEMBERS THIS ISSUE: $18.95

ISBN: 1-56661-000-1 (paper);
1-56661-001-X (hardback)

The Library of Congress has cataloged this serial publication as follows:

Alaska Geographic. v.1-
   [Anchorage, Alaska Geographic Society] 1972-
   v. ill. (part col.). 23 x 31 cm.
   Quarterly
   Official publication of The Alaska Geographic Society.
   Key title: Alaska geographic, ISSN 0361-1353.

   1. Alaska—Description and travel—1959-
   —Periodicals. I. Alaska Geographic Society.

F901.A266 917.98'04'505 72-92087

Library of Congress 75[79112] MARC-S

Contents

The Town that Gold Built 4
The Rush for Gold 8
White Pass and Yukon Route Railroad 28
After the Gold Rush 42
Klondike Gold Rush National Historical Park .. 80
Bibliography 77
Index 78

The Town That Gold Built

Waters of the Pacific Ocean thread between the islands of southeastern Alaska, an archipelago off a narrow shelf of land abutting the Coast Mountains. The jagged peaks and immense glaciers of these mountains pose a formidable barrier between the United States and Canada. Travel the ocean channels through Southeast in a route popularly known as the Inside Passage, sail northwest past the towns of Ketchikan, Wrangell, Petersburg and Juneau, north up Lynn Canal to Haines, continue even farther north to the head of Taiya Inlet, and reach the launching grounds for more than a century of travel through the mountains to the other side. Here at the foot of tall mountains in a stunningly scenic valley lies Skagway, a small Alaska town of about 700 people by the 1990 tally.

Modern Skagway is a curious mix — part tourist attraction, part national historic park, part port town. In summer, the town swells with visitors. In winter, the steady rumble of ore trucks marks time until the tourists return. The trucks carry lead and zinc from Canadian mines to the port, where the ore is shipped to Asian smelters. Mining and tourism anchor the town's economy.

That is because Skagway's identity hinges on what it used to be — a lawless gold rush town. Skagway's population exploded almost overnight during the 1897 stampede to Canada's Klondike gold fields. For a short time during the gold rush era, Skagway was the largest community in Alaska.

Today, tourists by the thousands chase gold rush ghosts through Skagway's historic downtown. Visitors stroll boardwalks and shop in restored turn-of-the-century buildings along Broadway. They mingle with legendary gold rush characters resurrected by able actors; Jefferson Randolph "Soapy" Smith, Skagway's infamous con artist and ruthless gang leader, still walks the streets, his nefarious doings more romantic with each retelling.

Skagway gained its nickname "Gateway to the Yukon" for good reason. Nestled in a long, slender valley at the northern edge of Taiya Inlet, Skagway is a port of entry for people and goods traveling over the Coast Mountains into interior Canada. It was founded for that purpose during the gold rush. Thousands of gold-seekers landed in Skagway to begin the arduous overland trek to Canada, through the mountains at White Pass above Skagway or over Chilkoot Pass, above the Indian fishing camp of Dyea three miles to the north.

This overview of Taiya Inlet at the upper end of Lynn Canal shows the relationship of Dyea to Skagway, visible at right center. Dyea, now mostly a ghost town but a booming center during the gold rush, is toward the upper right around both points at the extreme upper end of the inlet. (Harry M. Walker)

Today, Skagway continues to be an important transportation center. It has a small but busy port, and a railroad and highway that link it to neighboring British Columbia and Yukon Territory. Skagway, with its natural deep-water harbor, is interior Canada's most convenient and closest year-round access to the sea.

A far-sighted riverboat captain, William Moore, homesteaded along the Skagway River in 1887 with his son Bernard. He envisioned his new town of "Mooresville" as the entry point for the huge gold strike he felt was sure to come in the Yukon wilderness. The town's drawing card would be a wagon trail blazed through the forested mountains and over White Pass.

Much of what Moore dreamed came true, but it was largely wrought by the engineering genius of railroad builder Mike Heney. The plucky Heney led crews of disenchanted gold-seekers in punching a narrow-gauge railroad through the rugged mountains where few thought the iron horse could go. Completed to Whitehorse in 1900, the railroad saved Skagway from abandonment when the rush ended. It became the town's economic backbone. With it, Skagway grew into the tidewater port for interior Canada. Trains carried in food and other supplies, brought out minerals and transported passengers through much of this century.

During World War II, the military annexed the railroad to carry supplies into Canada for construction of the Alaska-Canada (Alcan) Highway and the Canada Oil (Canol) pipeline. The White Pass remained the only overland route from Skagway to the interior until 1978, when the Klondike Highway 2 was opened to Whitehorse and to what is now called the Alaska Highway. In 1982, the railroad shut down and with its closing went nearly half the jobs in Skagway. The White Pass and Yukon Route has since been revived as a passenger train, one of the nation's few narrow-gauge lines now operating. From its windows can occasionally be glimpsed the narrow footpath worn through the wilderness by gold-seekers long ago.

The gold rush brought Skagway its first tourists, wealthy travelers cruising the Inside Passage who wanted to see the outrageous gold rush spectacle. With the railroad came a sense of permanence to the community. The violence and lawlessness that ruled early on ended when town surveyor Frank Reid dispatched Soapy Smith in a shootout. Churches, fraternal and civic organizations took hold. People decided to stay. A profusion of flower and vegetable gardens cropped up. The town described by Canadian Mountie Sam Steele as "little better than a hell on earth...about the roughest place in the world" soon adopted a new persona. It became "Skagway, Garden City of Alaska."

Skagway residents avidly garden today, and the town is filled in summer with neatly groomed flower beds. But its gold rush past draws the tourists. In the past decade, since the town formed a visitors and convention bureau, its tourism business has more than doubled. Today, Skagway promotes itself as a terminus for the west coast cruise ship industry, and its residents graciously accommodate tourists by extending business hours far into the evening.

Modern Skagway recreates the frothy gaiety of the 1890s, without the confusion and tragedy that befell so many whose dreams of riches disappeared in the reality of fulfilling them. Visitors to modern Skagway experience the gold rush in relative comfort. They arrive by cruise ships, the state ferry or commuter airline out of Juneau, by car and train. Horse-drawn buggies provide taxi service around town. Relics of gold rush days abound, showcased in the Trail of '98 Museum and evidenced in the restored gold rush buildings that are part of the larger Klondike Gold Rush National Historical Park. Skagway also is the starting point for adventurers hiking the Chilkoot Pass trail, now maintained by the National Park Service. Visitors with their own automobiles or those on tour buses can travel the spectacularly scenic Klondike Highway 2. The refurbished White Pass and Yukon Route railroad also offers overland service during the summer.

What follows is the story of Skagway, from before it was Mooresville through its gold rush heyday, from its reign as Alaska's "Garden City" through its mini-boom during World War II and on into the present, a modern town where the glitter of gold is never far away.

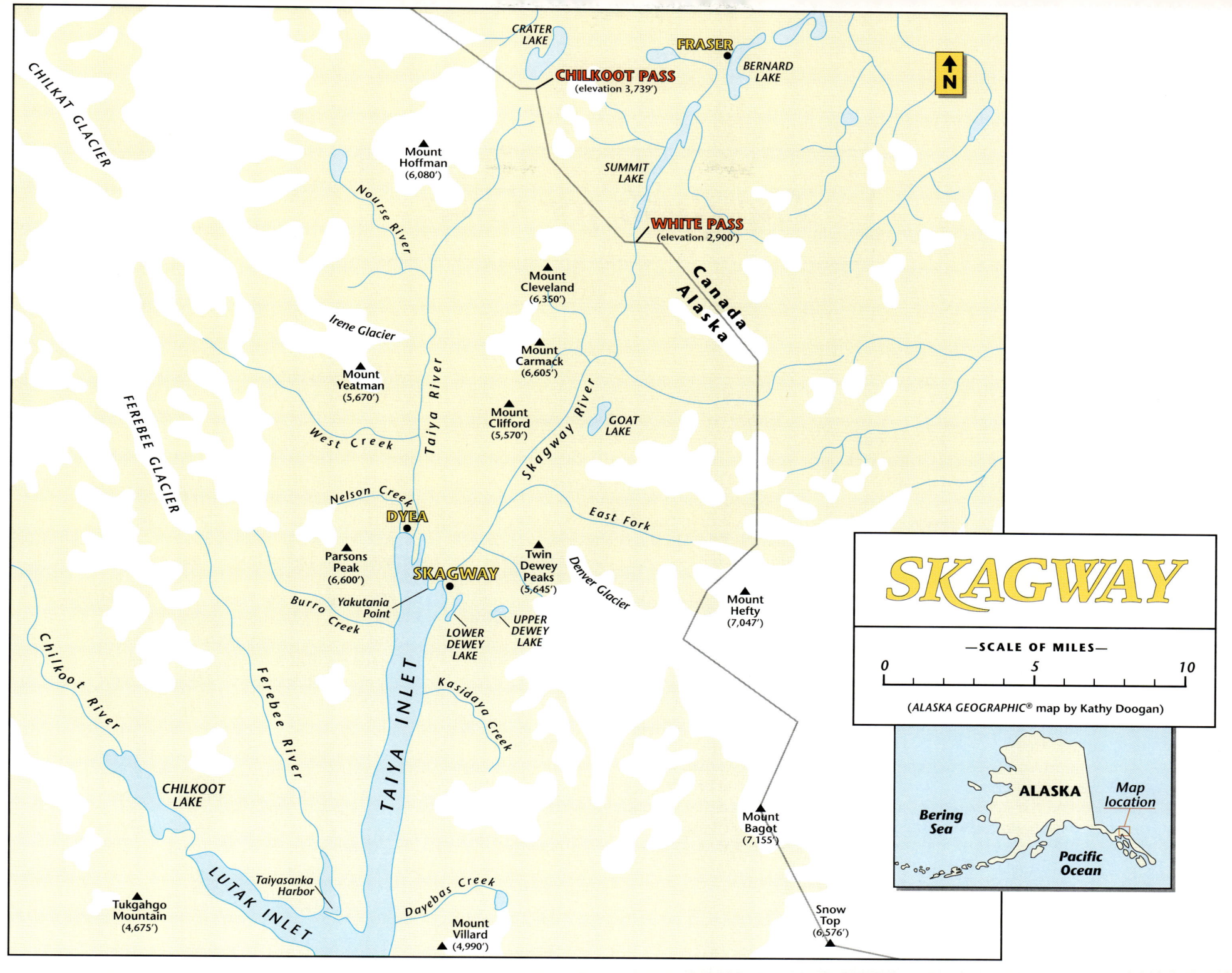

The Rush for Gold

The Klondike gold rush lasted less than three years, but it was a sensational, mad time in the nation's history. Accounts of its significance and its thousands of personal dramas fill volumes. Most include tales about the crazy gateway city of Skagway.

The gold rush created Skagway, and it altered the attitude of America. The industrial crash of 1893 had left millions of people jobless, their families near starvation. Severe economic depression gripped the nation. The country's supply of money was tied directly to reserves of gold, and a foreign drain on these reserves had induced a gold hoarding panic. Dollars were short, and credit almost impossible to get. Nothing indicated relief. Despair haunted the streets.

Then in midsummer 1897 came two ships from Alaska, the *Excelsior* to San Francisco and the *Portland* to Seattle. They carried tattered and dirty prospectors from the Klondike River valley with suitcases, bottles and moosehide pouches full of gold — nearly two tons. A special edition of the *Seattle Post-Intelligencer* told of nuggets the size of guinea eggs and prospectors who in two months had mined $150,000 worth of gold. "The stories they tell seem too incredulous and far beyond belief," reporter Beriah Brown wired from the ship steaming into Seattle. His dispatches also cautioned of hardships awaiting the unfit and ill-prepared.

But to a destitute populace, news of gold in the Klondike meant prospects of money in their pockets. Before the *Portland* reached shore, ticket offices were swamped with people of every description clamoring for space on the next ships north. The rush was on, and within weeks every available vessel joined the fleet, seaworthy or not. Men, women and children pressed shoulder to shoulder along the docks up and down the Pacific coast. Entrepreneurs hawked all sorts of wares, innovations such as evaporated potatoes, onions and eggs as well as useless contraptions like sail-powered bicycle-sleds. One company, writes Archie Satterfield in *Chilkoot Pass* (1973), offered gophers trained to claw holes in frozen ground. Meanwhile, west coast cities cashed in on the northward surge of fortune seekers, each town advertising nationwide as the port of entry to the Klondike. In reality, Skagway would be where the real journey began for many.

The Place of the Fierce North Wind

When gold fever hit, the town of Skagway did not exist. Instead, Mooresville occupied the flatlands of a steep-sided valley near the northeastern edge of Lynn

From a mud path lined with tents, Broadway Street became Skagway's main thoroughfare during the gold rush. This May 20, 1898, scene shows a bustling Broadway a month before the railroad came through town. (Anchorage Museum, Photo no. B64.1.21)

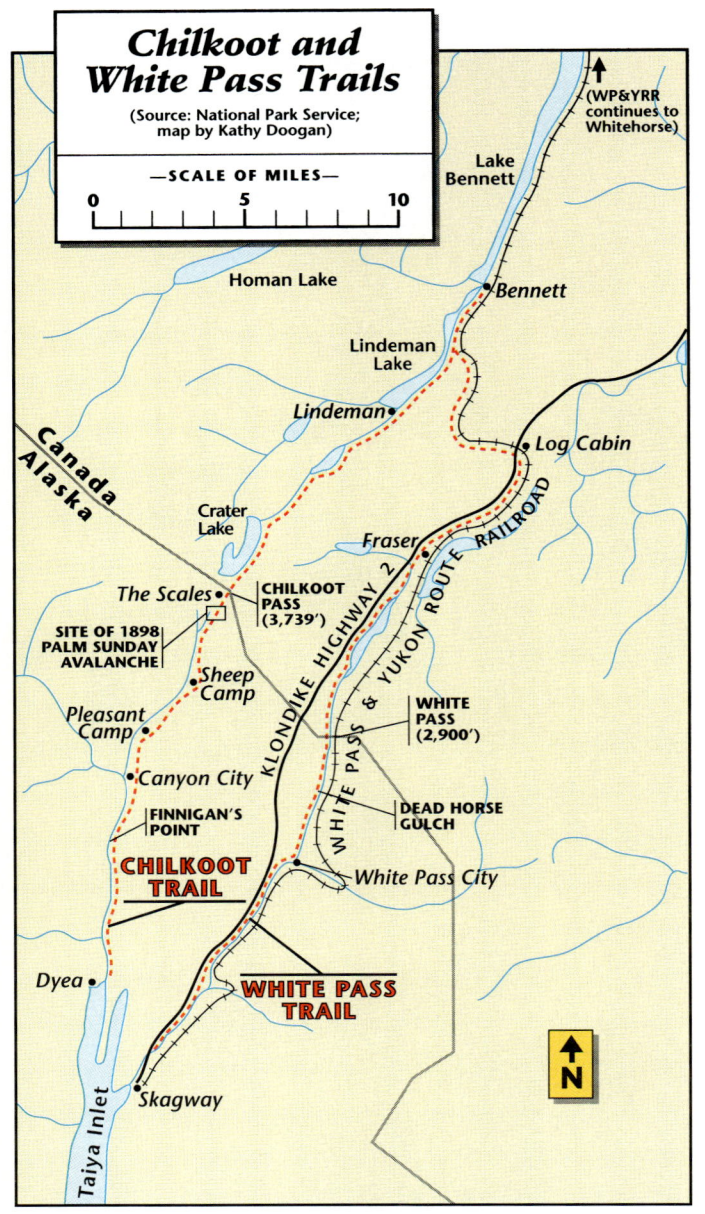

Canal. Mooresville was not much. It consisted of one log cabin, a small sawmill under construction, and a short wharf into Skagway Bay. Riverboat captain William Moore and his son Bernard had built the structures on a 160-acre homestead they had staked 10 years earlier, in 1887, along the Skagway River.

Moore figured a huge gold strike in the Yukon was coming; reports of limited finds had been trickling out of the region for more than two decades. He envisioned his town as the gateway to the gold fields through White Pass, a route familiar to Indians but only a rumor among whites. He blazed a narrow trail to the summit. He asked the Canadian and U.S. governments for toll road privileges over the pass. He intended to offer packing services over what he hoped would become a wagon road, or perhaps a railroad, to the Yukon River. From there he planned to operate steamboats to the gold fields.

The late historian William Bronson described Moore in *The Last Grand Adventure* (1977) as "a man with one of the most remarkable pioneer careers in the history of the West." His feats included, at age 74, snowshoeing nearly 700 miles through the interior in the dead of winter. He had fought in the Mexican War of 1846, then for the next 50 years tried to cash in on every Pacific coast gold rush from Peru to Canada. He piloted some of the first steamboats on British Columbia rivers. At the end of the Cassiar rush in British Columbia, his fleet of steamships bankrupt. In early 1887, he found himself in Alaska, employed by Canadian surveyor William Ogilvie.

Ogilvie had orders to locate the Canadian boundary across the Yukon River and along the Coast Mountains. Canada contended her jurisdiction extended to the head of Lynn Canal; the United States maintained Canada had no tidewater access and claimed its boundary north to Lake Bennett. An increasingly steady flow of prospectors, traders and trappers into the Far North had accelerated the boundary dispute. Each country sent surveyors to determine the international boundary.

Some of the traffic into the interior at this time came on the all-water route, by steamship around western Alaska to St. Michael and up the Yukon River. This route was 4,200 miles from Puget Sound to Dawson City, and was closed seven months a year by freeze-up on the Yukon. A few prospectors came into the country along a handful of overland routes. One of these routes traversed Chilkoot Pass in the mountains above the Taiya River estuary.

Chilkoot Pass for years had been the exclusive domain of the Chilkoot Indians, a band of coastal Tlingits. The Chilkoots dominated the trade with interior Dené Athabaskan Indians, primarily the Tagish tribe at Lake Bennett. These Dené were also called the Stick Indians because they lived in the land of forests, or sticks. The Chilkoots trekked from tidewater through the pass with seal oil, clam shells and dried fish to trade for the Dené's animal hides,

The small Indian village and trading post of Dyea, at the foot of the Chilkoot Pass trail, grew rapidly into one of Alaska's largest towns during the gold rush. At its height, the boomtown boasted a transient population of 8,000 to 10,000, with saloons, cafes, gambling parlors, stores, businesses and several hotels including the 115-room Olympic, then Alaska's largest. (Anchorage Museum, Photo no. B65.18.255)

furs, skin clothing and copper. After European contact in the early 19th century, the trade included calico, guns, flour and tobacco.

The first prospector — and perhaps the first white man — to cross Chilkoot Pass was George Holt in 1878, although little is known of how he slipped past the hostile Indians guarding the route. United States naval officer Lester A. Beardslee is credited with opening the pass to white prospectors in 1880, reinforcing the treaty with a demonstration of his ship's Gatling gun.

Within the next several years, many white prospectors traveled the Chilkoot, paying Tlingits to carry their supplies. The Indians soon realized a substantial profit and let go of their interior trade to monopolize the lucrative packing business. U.S. Army Lt. Frederick Schwatka employed Indian packers over the pass in 1883, during a reconnaissance mission into Yukon Territory. His trip, among other things, popularized the route by providing the first survey. At the time, the Indians charged $9 to $12 for each hundred pounds, a rate that escalated with later demand. Schwatka said afterward he "in no way blamed the Indians for their stubbornness in maintaining what seemed at first to be exorbitant, and only wondered that they would do this extremely fatiguing labor so reasonably."

In 1886, partners John J. Healy and Edgar Wilson opened a trading post at the foot of the Chilkoot Pass trail, on the banks of the Dyea River. The name comes from the Tlingit word *Diyéi*, meaning "to pack." The Tlingits had long maintained a camp here, from which they controlled the trail and fished. Most of the Indian villages were along the Chilkat River to the west, where fishing was better, but some families frequented the Dyea River during fall salmon runs and eventually settled here.

Healy brought his shrewd and daring brand of frontier business acumen to play in Dyea. During days of running a whiskey fort on the Montana-Canada border, he had quelled a take-over attempt by holding a lighted cigar over a keg of gunpowder and threatening to blow up the entire group, himself included. Healy drifted to the interior and formed the North American Trading and Transportation Co. to compete with the Alaska Commercial Co. on the Yukon River at Fortymile. With the increasing number of prospectors filtering over Chilkoot Pass, he saw opportunity at Dyea, and hired George Dickson, who had lived among the Chilkats, as storekeeper and translator.

When Ogilvie and his survey party with Captain Moore reached Dyea in 1887, Ogilvie reported 138 Indians, Dickson, and Healy and his wife living here. Ogilvie proceeded with his mission into the interior. But Moore had another agenda. One of his two sons, who were prospecting in the Yukon Valley, had sent word of a secret pass through the mountains nearby. The alternate route was said to be lower in altitude with a gentler grade that would allow pack animals through, something impossible on the scree- and boulder-covered Chilkoot with its 35-degree slope. Moore determined to find that pass.

Ogilvie also had heard reports of it while in Juneau. He was weary of Moore's obsessive ravings, and gladly released him to find it. The Chilkoots acted dumb about the pass when questioned, to protect their business out of Dyea. Finally, Moore persuaded a Tagish Indian in camp, a man known as Skookum (strong) Jim Mason, to show him the way.

From Skagway Bay, some three miles south of Dyea, Moore and Skookum Jim spent seven June days hacking their way to the summit. They tangled with dense underbrush, fought swarms of mosquitoes, forded swollen rivers and creeks, and picked their way around rocky bluffs. Moore measured the trail at 18 zigzagging, rollercoaster miles from the alluvial plain at tidewater to the top. He reported his findings to Ogilvie when they met at Lake Lindeman. Ogilvie named the pass White, after Thomas White, Canadian Minister of the Interior who authorized the survey. Moore, who had considerable experience building roads through the mountains, was convinced more than ever that the route was suitable for a wagon road or a railroad.

Captain Moore remained with the Ogilvie party until they met up with Moore's son Bernard two months later on the Yukon River. The elder Moore confided his desire to settle the foot of White Pass. The two bade the others

Travelers are ready to leave Skagway for the 600-mile run to Dawson City, center of the Klondike gold fields. The usual route was up the Skagway River valley, then over White Pass to upper tributaries of the Yukon River, and down the river to Dawson. (Courtesy of Mrs. James Doogan)

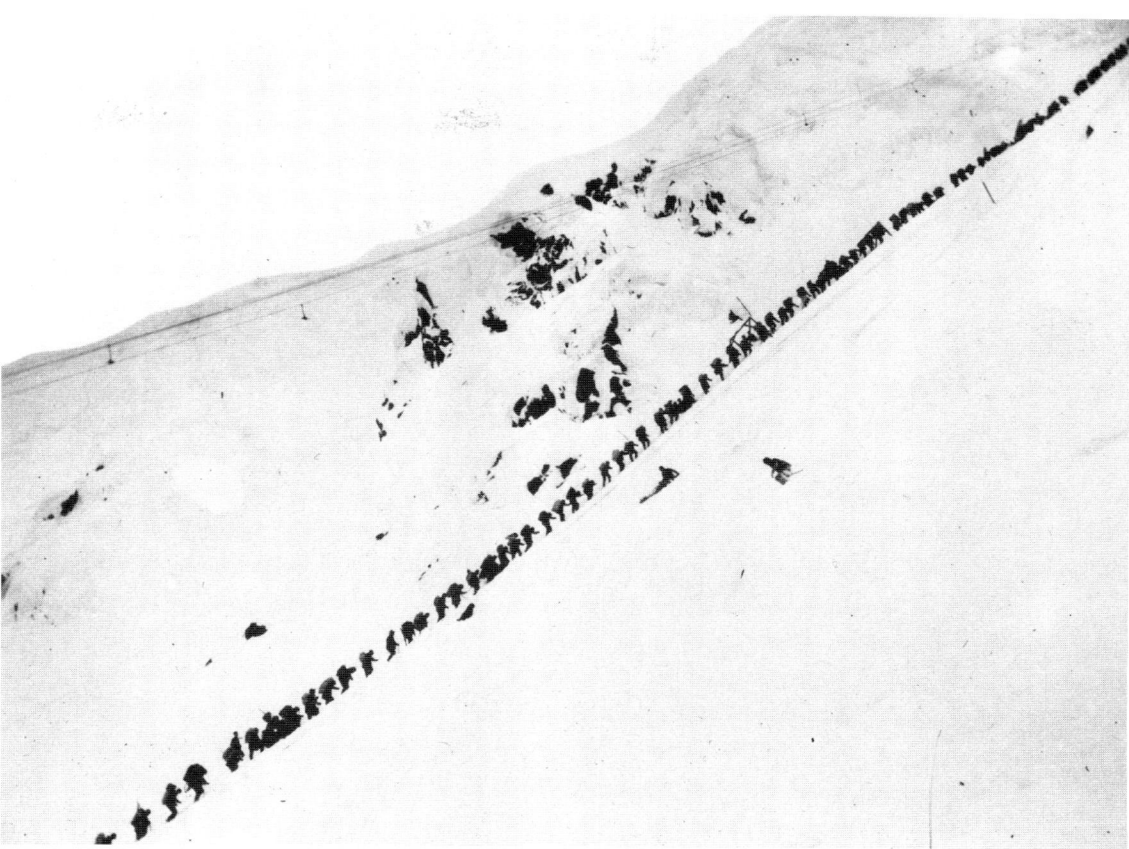

One of the most famous images to come out of the gold rush is that of gold-seekers toiling step by step up the steep approach to the summit of Chilkoot Pass. They had to make several trips to ferry their supplies up the 35-degree slope, then over the summit and on to Lake Lindeman, start of the river route that would eventually carry them to the Klondike gold fields. (Canadian Government Office of Tourism)

goodbye and headed out of the interior.

In October, they landed at Skagway Bay in a canoe full of supplies obtained at Juneau. "I have never forgotten my father's words to me," Bernard wrote years later in *Skagway In Days Primeval* (1968).

" 'Here,' he said, 'we will cast our future lots and try to hew out our fortune.' My father also said on this occasion: 'I fully expect before many years to see a pack trail through this pass, followed by a wagon road, and I would not be at all surprised to see a railroad through to the lakes.'"

It would take work. The valley had been formed in the retreat of glaciers some 10,000 years earlier and was thick with poplars, spruce and wild game, including bear. Chilling winds funneled off the glaciers from the north and up Lynn Canal from the south. The Tlingit place name *Shagagwei* "would require our English word 'wind' to be used frequently," wrote Bernard. "Skagway is a name very typical of a place where the same air is never breathed twice."

No Indians lived in permanent villages here when the Moores arrived, although Bernard found old campsites, ax blades, deadfall traps and a weathered, half-finished cottonwood canoe. An Indian named Wausuck was camped at Smuggler's Cove off Skagway Bay. Modern day Tlingits recall stories of their ancestors hunting mountain goats in the peaks above Skagway Valley. Remnants of prehistoric sites recently found by archaeologists include one at Smuggler's Cove and two small shell middens, one at Yakutania Point and one near Dyea. Historians speculate that the Indians may have not settled the Skagway Valley because of cold north winds and lack of good fishing — the silty Skagway River drained gulches leading to White Pass and did not support a strong salmon run.

The Moores, which later included Bernard's Tlingit wife and children, spent

ALASKA GEOGRAPHIC® 13

By March 1898, Brackett's wagon road was open to White Pass City, four miles below the summit. Many packers and freighters traveled the river when it was frozen to avoid paying Brackett's tolls. From White Pass City to the summit, a narrow pack-train trail ascended steeply 1,000 feet. (Anchorage Museum, Photo no. B64.1.25)

parts of the next decade working on their homestead. Captain Moore incessantly promoted Mooresville, but got disparaging remarks instead of financial support. He returned to steamshipping in British Columbia and held a government mail contract to earn some money. Bernard worked at sawmills and mines around Douglas. In 1895, Bernard convinced seven men from California to cross into the Yukon through White Pass, the first party of miners to do so. Finally, Captain Moore secured from investor E.E. Billinghurst about $1,800 in supplies, animals, lumber and wages for summer 1896. As they readied Mooresville, a gold strike was in the making on the creeks of the Klondike River.

The first big find came August 1896 on Rabbit Creek, later to be renamed Bonanza. Skookum Jim, who had led Moore over White Pass, made the find although it was credited to his hunting companion and brother-in-law George Washington Carmack. Carmack convinced him that an Indian would never be allowed to record the claim. He gave Jim half-interest in return for right of ownership. Carmack carried out the gold in a Winchester rifle cartridge to the mining town of Fortymile and registered his claims, precipitating a mini-stampede. A larger one followed from Circle City, 220 miles below the mouth of the Klondike, when news reached there about two months later. The second creek staked was Eldorado, which joined Bonanza. By spring 1897, news filtered down to the West Coast and the first wave of gold-seekers left for the Klondike.

It was pay dirt washed from the sands of the Bonanza, Eldorado and nearby creeks that the *Excelsior* and the *Portland* carried on their world-startling journey to the states. Six days after the *Portland* arrived, the steamship *Queen* headed out of Seattle with a load of eager prospectors bound for northern riches. The ship steamed into Dyea, but Bernard Moore persuaded the captain to backtrack to Mooresville and unload. *The Islander, George W. Elder* and *Willamette* soon followed.

Madness at Skagway

Moore's dream for Mooresville abruptly ended with these boatloads of adventurers. They washed ashore like the inlet's 25-foot tide, drowning Moore's indignant proclamations of ownership in a wave of greed. And for many of them, their dreams ended too, but in a different way and for different reasons.

A tent city popped up overnight. The Moores tried to collect rent from the squatters, but were ignored. In early August, stampeders gathered to organize their new town, which they named Skagway. They appointed Frank Reid, an ex-school teacher from Sweet Home, Ore., who was tending bar in a tent, to be town surveyor and selected Commissioner John U. Smith as recorder. Reid platted the town, and within a few days Smith had made more than 1,100 entries.

Moore's residence happened to sit in the middle of one of the new intersections. The Captain refused to move. While his wife sobbed inside, Moore stood on his porch waving a crow bar at the wrecking crew who judiciously backed off. But Moore realized that for all practical purposes Mooresville was dead. He bought a lot, moved his residence and took his fight to U.S. District Court. Four years later, he was awarded 25 percent of the assessed valuation of improvements on his homestead.

Newcomers continued pouring into Skagway. Moore realized the gateway city was still flush with promise, extended his wharf into deeper water and made a small fortune producing lumber at his sawmill.

During the first months of the stampede, order in Skagway resembled little more than anarchy. Naturalist John Muir visited and refused a magazine's request to describe the scene. He said the gold rush looked like a hill of ants someone had stirred up with a stick.

Others were not as kind. "Skagway was the boiling pot of Hell," wrote Eugene Allen, publisher of Dawson City's *Klondike Nugget*, "where were assembled the dregs of the earth and woe unto the stampeder

An immense tent camp sprouted almost overnight on the shores of Lake Bennett during the gold rush. After having traversed White Pass or Chilkoot Pass, gold-seekers camped at the lake, building boats and preparing for their trip downriver to Dawson and the gold fields. (Alaska State Library, P.E. Larss Collection, Photo No. PCA 41-21; reprinted from ALASKA GEOGRAPHIC®)

who failed to attend strictly to his business of stampeding."

Annie Hall Strong, a female stampeder, recalled her arrival in Skagway in an October 1897 issue of *The Skaguay News*. "[J]udging from the terrible tales told by returning and disheartened gold seekers, I was to fall among the riff-raff of the whole country at a place called Skaguay....Cutthroats and mobs of evil-doers were said to form the population, and it was alleged that they lay in wait for the arrival of 'tenderfeet.'

"On the morning of the 26th of August we steamed around a point into a bay and right before us lay the beautifully situated little tented town. It looked peaceful enough from the deck of the steamship *Queen*, but the faces of the future Eldorado kings looked anxious and for once I remained behind...thinking I would postpone my entrance into this modern Sodom until it became compulsory.

"Towards evening, with fear and dread, I ventured ashore. To my surprise I found a surging crowd of people busy as bees rushing hither and thither — but everything was orderly and quiet...."

The natural beauty of the place — mountains rising into azure peaks out of a valley lush with cottonwood, spruce, hemlock and birch, edged on the west side by the swift, milky river — undoubtedly was lost on most arrivals. Some would-be miners took one look at the steep mountains and sold their supplies for a ticket home.

Newspaperman Elmer "Stroller" White, who worked at *The Skaguay News* briefly before heading on to Dawson, wrote of a tent restaurant opened by one miner trying to finance his exodus home. By midmorning, the proprietor had sold enough hotcakes to buy a ticket to Seattle. He sold his restaurant to another fellow who kept it through the lunch hour, then sold it to a third party. That man owned it long enough to serve dinner before losing it in a gambling game.

Most of the gold-seekers, however, plunged ahead on the arduous overland journey. First they had to sort their provisions from heaps of supplies dumped on muddy beaches in the frenzy to unload the ships. Until wharves were built into deep water at both Skagway and Dyea, the stampeders paid to have their supplies lightered by scow or canoe, often times pushing their horses overboard to swim to shore. Sometimes they waded ashore themselves with their goods, staggering through knee-deep mud and into holes that dunked them up to their armpits.

Edwin Tappan Adney, the Klondike correspondent for *Harper's Weekly*, described the scene in August 1897: "There are great crowds of men rowing in boats to the beach, then clambering out in rubber boots and packing the stuff, and setting it down in little piles out of reach of the tide. Horses are tethered out singly and in groups. Tents there are of every size and kind.... Behind these are more tents and men, and piles of merchandise and hay, bacon smoking, men loading bags and bales of hay upon horses and starting off...in the direction of a grove of small cottonwoods, beyond which lies the trail toward White Pass....All is movement and action. There is nothing fixed. The tent of yesterday is a wooden building today....No one pretends to follow the changes that are going on here. Those who have been here a week are old-timers. When the next boat arrives people will ask questions of us in turn."

The more affluent paid Indian packers or horse packers to haul their provisions. Others shouldered their loads a hundred pounds at a time from cache to cache. This backbreaking relay would stretch their walk to 2,500 miles by the time they reached Bennett or Lindeman lakes on the other side. Hardworking stampeders might take three months to reach the lakes, where they built boats for the trip down treacherous waterways to the gold fields.

The risks of going for gold — storms, avalanches, cliff-hanging trails slick with mud or ice, accidents, diseases, rotten food,

Skagway has a tradition of outlandish parades. The town's first Fourth of July parade in 1898 was a grand affair headed by Soapy Smith on a prancing white horse. Soapy may well have been the most experienced grand marshal in Skagway. Only two months earlier, he had led a Memorial Day parade of Smith's Alaska Guards, men whom he had enlisted to fight in the just-started Spanish American War. The men, wearing homemade ribbon and butcher-paper badges, marched around town to the music of a brass band. Outside the Princess Hotel the parade leaders were swarmed by the madam Babe Davenport and her girls in their working uniforms although, noted newspaperman Elmer "Stroller" White, "what they wore for uniforms was barely visible to the naked eye." They wanted Smith to form a Ladies Auxiliary, but he pushed them aside and continued the parade to his saloon, where he gave a rousing patriotic speech and invited in the troops for drinks — at a profit of about $2,500. The war department subsequently declined the service of Soapy's guards. (Anchorage Museum; Photo no. B64.1.44)

no food, theft, murder, suicide — would have deterred more reasonable souls. But gold fever induced lemminglike behavior. Of the 100,000 people whom historians say started out for the Klondike, 24,000 to 40,000 made it over the passes toting some 60 million pounds of goods.

Going for the Summit

"This trail – its winding in and out
Leaves one's mind in serious doubt
Whether man who planned this route
Was going to Hell or coming out."

— Blazed on a spruce tree on the White Pass trail, from the diary of Florence Hartshorn, wife of blacksmith at Log Cabin, a camp on the Canadian side

There was nothing easy about getting to the Klondike. The prospectors who came up the Inside Passage and landed at Skagway had two choices: the White Pass trail or the Chilkoot Pass trail. There were a number of other routes — over Valdez Glacier from Prince William Sound, over Malaspina Glacier from Yakutat, up the Stikine River from Wrangell, the all-Canadian route from Edmonton, or by boat up the Yukon River from St. Michael. But nine out of 10 stampeders that first year passed through Skagway or Dyea, according to late historian William Bronson in *The Last Grand Adventure*.

The Chilkoot Pass trail was the older, better-established route, but that was about all there was to recommend it. It was shorter, only 14 miles to the summit, but higher at 3,500 feet. The last four miles ascended steeply amid loose scree and boulders. In winter, this stretch became a nearly vertical set of steps carved in the snow. Some of the most famous gold rush pictures were taken here at the Golden Stairs, showing the antlike column of miners toiling to the top. These steps, famous as they were, were a one-time occurrence, during March and April 1898. Two brothers improved them and charged a toll. The Chilkoot was said to be too steep for pack animals, but some of the earliest prospectors did not know that. They put their horses in rope slings and hoisted them over on their sides.

The newer, lesser-known White Pass trail was advertised as the freighter's choice. The route was nine miles longer but the summit was some 700 feet lower, and its promoters promised all-weather, easy passage for pack trains. But the trail was not much. The narrow footpath blazed by Moore was quickly churned into a mucky mess. Its steep stretches became slick mud chutes. Part of the trail hung between steep cliffs and yawning ravines with little room to maneuver. Miners who stopped to rest or adjust their loads might wait hours before a break appeared in the traffic and they could rejoin the procession.

"Discouraged men are coming down from the trail, and they have but one story to tell — of terrible hardship," wrote Adney, one of the first journalists over the trail. "The road, if it can be called a road, in terrible condition...most of them regret having started....That the advertising of the Skagway trail as the better route was premature no one pretends to dispute — nay, it is only in terms of unqualified condemnation that it may be mentioned. Those who cut that trail may have honestly believed it to be better, but the effect of rains and of thousands of men and horses tramping to and fro was not foreseen."

But was the Chilkoot any better during those first months of the stampede? No one seemed to know even then. One sourdough who had traveled both told Adney: "Whichever way you go, you will wish you had gone the other."

Travel up each was made from camp to camp. From Dyea, the miners on the Chilkoot Pass Trail could boat or use pack animals up the Taiya River to Finnigan's Point, where Pat Finnigan and his two sons briefly charged a toll to use their corduroy bridge and road. During fall 1897, the settlement consisted of 75 tents, a blacksmith shop, saloon and restaurant.

A few miles farther, near the mouth of the Nourse River, was Canyon City. By May 1898, after construction of the

Skagway's strategic location near a pass through the Coast Mountains has made its waterfront a busy place since the gold rush. This 1901 view shows from left: a small portion of the Seattle Skagway Wharf, the Juneau Wharf, Alaska Southern Wharf and Moore's Wharf to which the cruise ship is tied. (Anchorage Museum, Photo no. B72.27.24)

tramways started, Canyon City grew to more than 1,500 people with streets, electric lights and at least 24 businesses. After rough going through Dyea Canyon, at mile 10 on the trail, the ground leveled into Pleasant Camp where there was a toll bridge across the Taiya River. By April 1898, tents continued almost without a break to Sheep Camp, at the beginning of the long climb to the summit. At its peak, Sheep Camp boasted 16 hotels, 14 restaurants, 13 supply houses, five doctors, three saloons, two dance halls, a post office and 6,000 to 8,000 people.

The next stop, The Scales, was known as the most wretched spot on the trail. This is where packers would reweigh their loads and up their rates for the summit. Many discouraged and penniless prospectors gave up here. Those who continued tackled The Golden Stairs, a 35-degree climb to the summit. One trip took up to six hours, and some stampeders needed 30 trips to move their gear across the pass.

The scene at the narrow passage of the Chilkoot summit was one of vast piles of freight, shouting men and howling winds. Workers at 10 tent hotels, and at tent restaurants and customs brokerages sheltered, fed and counted the gold-seekers. Telephone and postal services were also available.

The North West Mounted Police collected customs at the summits, and by the end of the first winter, they required any miner entering Canada to have a year's supply of food.

Along with the recommended staples — 350 pounds of flour, 150 pounds of bacon, 100 pounds of beans, 100 pounds of sugar — came a smorgasbord of more unusual items. One couple toted a piano over the Chilkoot. They wrapped the sounding board in yarn for protection, and when they reached their destination, the woman knitted sweaters from the yarn and sold them at a profit. Another woman carried yeast bread dough on her back, the dough rising from the heat of her body and ready to bake at night. Two wealthy society ladies took along their pets, a music box and a portable bowling alley. One of the stranger sights on the White Pass trail was a flock of 100 turkeys herded over the pass by a couple of enterprising chaps who were off to sell them at Dawson.

Most of the time, the stampede was drudgery and tragedy all too frequent.

In September 1897, just after the rush began, an ice dam above the Chilkoot trail broke and released a torrent of water that swept through Sheep Camp. Only one man died, but the flood washed many people out of their tents and ruined tons of gear.

In summer 1898 Skagway citizens tired of Soapy Smith's shenanigans. Soapy died in a shootout with town surveyor Frank Reid, and members of his gang were rounded up in front of City Hall. (Courtesy of Mrs. James Doogan)

Promoters' claims that the White Pass trail posed no difficulties for pack animals were less than accurate. Writer Jack London traveled the trail in fall 1897 and recalled the scene later in The God of His Fathers, Tales of the Klondike and the Yukon *(1902): The horses died like mosquitoes in the first frost and from Skagway to Bennett they rotted in heaps. They died at the rocks, they were poisoned at the summit, and they starved at the lakes; they fell off the trail, what there was of it, and they went through it; in the river they drowned under their loads or were smashed to pieces against the boulders; they snapped their legs in the crevices and they sank from fright or smothered in the slime; and they were disembowelled in the bogs where the corduroy logs turned end up in the mud; men shot them, worked them to death and when they were gone, went back to the beach and bought more. Some did not bother to shoot them, stripping the saddles off and the shoes and leaving them where they fell. Their hearts turned to stone — those which did not break — and they became beasts, the men on the Dead Horse Trail.*
(Anchorage Museum, Photo no. B64.1.34)

A series of snowstorms followed by warm weather in March created conditions on the same trail for the Palm Sunday avalanche of 1898. The Indian packers refused to work and sourdoughs on the trail warned of danger, but the gold-seekers wanted to make good use of the clear spell. About 10:30 the morning of April 3, the mountainside slid away, taking as many as 70 miners with it. Some 1,500 rescuers immediately started digging people out from 30 feet of snow. "The voices of the entombed reached me from all directions," recalled a survivor, Mr. Black, in the April 9, 1898, issue of *The Dyea Trail*. "Many seemed to be praying and some were saying good-bye to relatives at home. It was the most ominous and impressive time of my life." Many of those found dead were taken to the Slide Cemetery at Dyea. All that spring, melting snow uncovered more bodies along the trail.

One of the most chronicled legacies of the gold rush was the cruel treatment of horses on the White Pass trail. Many horses were overloaded, overworked and underfed. Their backs were rubbed raw and bloody by ill-fitting packs put on by men who had no idea what they were doing. Sharp rocks on the trail cut the horses' feet until they staggered in pain. There were a few packers who treated their horses right, fed them adequately, shod them properly and never lost an animal. But thousands of horses died during the fall and winter of 1897, and the stony path up slippery Devil's Hill and boulder-strewn Porcupine Hill became known as Dead Horse Trail. Carcasses of dead animals in the gulches below rotted to a ghastly stench the next summer.

John Sydney Webb wrote in the March 1898 issue of *Century Magazine*: "Many animals died from exhaustion; but by far the greater number were destroyed

by falling among boulders, the heavy packs nearly always causing broken limbs…so warped had men become in their struggle to get over the summits… that no friendly hand would be lent to help the owner raise the fallen animal."

Samuel Graves, president of the White Pass railway that eventually would replace the need for pack horses, told of a horse with a broken leg mercifully killed with an ax to its head. "Traffic on the trail was resumed across the still-warm body of the horse," he later recalled. That night "there wasn't a vestige of the carcass left. The head was on one side of the trail and the tail on the other. The beast was ground into the earth by the trampling feet of the human machine…."

Adney wrote in disbelief: "Yesterday a horse deliberately walked over the face of Porcupine Hill. Said one of the men who saw it: 'It looked to me, sir, like suicide. I don't know but that I'd rather commit suicide too, than be driven by some of the men on this trail.'"

Mining Skagway

As each ship brought hundreds of newcomers striking out for the pass, a number of prospectors realized their Eldorado in the various towns along the way. They set up shops to serve the dizzying flood of newcomers, instituting a degree of order in chaos.

The Feero pack train starts for Lake Bennett in 1898. John E. Feero came north from Tacoma, Wash. in August 1897. He and his wife, Emma Babcock Feero, had come to Washington state from Maine in 1889. Another packer, Joe Brooks, hired Feero for $5 per day because he was an experienced horseman. Feero became disgusted at the way the Brooks crew treated pack animals, and formed his own packing company. He died during a storm in December 1898. (Courtesy of Mrs. James Doogan)

Newsboys for The Skaguay News *line up in 1898. Frank Feero, son of packer John Feero, is second from left. (Courtesy of Mrs. James Doogan)*

Within three months of the first arrivals, *The Skaguay News* boasted that the town had 3,000 residents and 700 wooden or tent structures. Its businesses included 15 general merchandise stores, 19 restaurants, 16 hotels and lodging houses, six real estate offices, seven doctors, six lawyers, three dentists, two barbers, two dressmakers, three laundries, six lumber yards and a sawmill, eight pack trains, 11 blacksmiths and an equal number of feed yards, four meat markets, three wharves, a bowling alley and three typewriters.

An October edition of *The Skaguay News* predicted the town's population at 10,000 in two years; three months later, it upped its forecast to 50,000 to 100,000. Promoters optimistically touted Skagway as the San Francisco of the North.

But their claims of civility ignored the notorious reputation Skagway was rapidly gaining at the hands of racketeer Soapy Smith.

Soapy arrived in Skagway in fall 1897 with five henchmen and quickly established his crime syndicate. A dapperly dressed gent, he posed as a businessman and philanthropist while masterminding scams to fleece gold-seekers. He recruited a posse of outlaws to do his dirty deals. They dressed well and appeared reputable. He supposedly was in cahoots with several of the town's more influential citizens, including town recorder Judge Smith and the editor of the *Daily Alaskan*, and no one was quite sure who worked for him. His men walked the docks, cheerfully directing newcomers to any number of bogus storefronts, like the Information Bureau. From there, they were steered to other shams, like Reliable Packers or the Merchant's Exchange. One of Soapy's more ingenious shake-downs was the Telegraph Office, where the operator would send a message anywhere in the world for $5. Answers would come back in a matter of

This 1910 photo shows Edith Feero, one of John Feero's twin daughters, and her husband, Carl Larson, a carpenter at the White Pass and Yukon Route railroad. Their son Stewart, now retired, became a railroad engineer in Washington state. Edith died January 25, 1981, at age 93. (Courtesy of Mrs. James Doogan)

In gold rush years, the easiest way to get from Skagway to Dyea was by boat. Here the Florence *carries (from left) Guy Sipprell, Ethel Black, Edna Black and Bill Wright. (Courtesy of Mrs. James Doogan)*

hours, always collect. The office did a booming business despite the fact that Skagway had no telegraph lines at the time.

Even though liquor manufacture and sales were prohibited in Alaska, Skagway had saloons — some accounts say as many as 70 — and a number of breweries. Barrels of whiskey cleared at the docks for transport to Canada invariably contained nothing but water by the time they reached the border. Soapy allegedly headed the whiskey cartel.

His men roamed up and down the Chilkoot and White Pass trails, running gambling and liquor tents and stealing what they could. Their shenanigans stopped at the summits, where the North West Mounted Police patrolled the border from customs posts. Soapy also was smart enough to leave the townspeople alone. But his plethora of confidence games entrapped unsuspecting passers-through.

There were gambling houses galore — including Soapy's own Jeff's Parlor — where miners would invariably lose at shell games, faro and the all-time favorite, poker. And there were hurdy gurdy girls, dance-hall queens like Ethel the Moose, the Montana Filly and Mollie Fewclothes, and other "entertainers" who stripped their newly rich boyfriends to poverty in single-room row houses known as "the line."

Alexander MacDonald, an Englishman who passed through Skagway in fall 1897, said: "I have stumbled upon a few tough corners of the globe during my wanderings beyond the outposts of civilization, but I think the most outrageously lawless quarter I ever struck was Skagway....It seemed as if the scum of the earth had hastened here to fleece and rob, or...to murder."

Frontier traveler Henry Toke Munn wrote: "For the six nights I slept in Skagway there was shooting on the streets every night. At least one man was killed that I knew of and probably others. The shack I slept in had a bullet through it over my head."

Finally in summer 1898, Skagway's citizenry had had enough. The Committee of 101, a group of men who earlier had tried to curb Soapy, revived to avenge the robbery of prospector John Stewart. Stewart had come off the trail headed home to Seattle with some $2,500 worth of gold dust in his poke. A couple of Soapy's men engaged him in conversation and suggested he stash his gold in the hotel's safe overnight. It disappeared, of course, and the committee charged Smith

Skagway pioneers took advantage of the berry patches that were sprinkled throughout the valley. George Black, second from left, gathers his friends for a berry-picking outing near town in the early 1900s. (Courtesy of Mrs. James Doogan)

with its return by that afternoon.

According to newspaper accounts from the time, an intoxicated Smith, armed with a Winchester rifle, staggered toward the wharf where the vigilante committee was meeting that night. Smith approached town surveyor Frank Reid, posted as lookout. The two men exchanged words and Smith jabbed Reid with the barrel of his gun. Reid drew his revolver with one hand while pushing away Smith's rifle with the other. Smith pulled the trigger, the shot hitting Reid's groin. Reid fired three shots, one passing through Smith's heart. Smith fired another shot before dropping dead. Reid died 12 days later, acclaimed the hero of Skagway.

Sibling Rivalry

Dyea boomed, too. Healy and Wilson's trading post had prospered early on with arrival of the first steamships of miners in spring 1897, when news of the Carmack strike first filtered out of the interior. The miners automatically headed for the well-known Chilkoot Pass trail.

They were met by Tlingit Indians who drove hard bargains for their packing services. The men were short, heavy-set and powerfully built with stringy black mustaches and scant beards. The women's faces were painted jet black or chocolate brown, rubbed with balsam, burned punk and grease, reported journalist Adney. The women and young boys packed 75-pound loads while the Indian men routinely carried 150 pounds or more.

By mid-December 1897, Dyea grew to 1,200 people, many of them late arrivals forced to wait until the spring thaw opened interior waterways to the Klondike. Crews cleared stumps to make streets, and construction began on a system of tramways to haul goods to the summit. Contractors worked around the clock building hotels, offices, warehouses and stores, and by spring Dyea had nearly 4,000 residents. It also had a church, a school, a public library and a literary society.

"Dyea has everything that every other town in Alaska has, except Soapy Smith," wrote the short-lived *Dyea Press*. In May 1898, a second wharf was completed; the first one on the west side of Dyea Inlet was inconvenient and never popular. The weekly *The Dyea Trail* boasted that the town had "the finest system of wharves and warehouses in all Alaska...at the mouth of the Chilkoot pass, the only route to the greatest gold fields known to history."

An intense rivalry erupted between Dyea and Skagway, fueled by the towns' newspapers. *The Dyea Trail* trumpeted the advantages of the Chilkoot Trail and Dyea, while casting aspersions on Skagway. "Poor Sister Skagway. She is always in trouble," the paper sarcastically lamented. Dyea's papers publicized the deadly spinal meningitis outbreak on the White Pass trail, as well as a riot on the Skagway waterfront; a steamship company tried to break a longshoremen's strike by using Indians to unload their boats. Skagway's lawlessness also received considerable coverage by the Dyea papers, even though Dyea was not without its share of crime.

The enterprising young city scored several coups. The North West Mounted Police switched from using the White Pass route to the Chilkoot to supply their posts in the Yukon. Also, Dyea businessmen diverted 500 travelers from Skagway.

Dyea may have had its trams, but Skagway was getting the Brackett wagon road to White Pass. *The Skaguay News* vociferously defended its trail against detractors. It railed against reports from Outside newspapers, particularly the "deliberate and malicious lies" published in the *Seattle Post-Intelligencer.* Meanwhile, the disastrous avalanche on the Chilkoot trail generated adverse publicity. Skagway businessmen held up the disaster as a solemn warning against using Dyea.

In May 1898, construction on the White Pass and Yukon Route railroad began. At first, Dyea scoffed.

"Good bye old Skag, good bye," wrote the *Trail* in May 1898. "A few railroad ties and a lot of talk will not build railroads. Beside which there is now no pressing need for one...the future belongs to Dyea...."

But by August, when Skagway's population was nearing 10,000 and the railroad was en route to the summit, the *Trail*'s tone mellowed. In a 40-page special edition, the *Trail* extolled both routes and congratulated Skagway on its railroad, suggesting that both towns could enjoy continued prosperity. But the railroad was the beginning of the end for Dyea.

In 1909, Edna Black (left), Guy Sipprell, Grandma Black, unidentified, Ethel Black and Vic Sparks picnic at Dyea, gold rush rival to Skagway. Dyea languished after the railroad was completed from Skagway to Whitehorse. (Courtesy of Mrs. James Doogan)

White Pass and Yukon Route Railroad

The draw of the gold fields sparked all sorts of big plans for controlling transportation into the Yukon. Investors proposed railroads north from British Columbia toward the gold fields, tramways over the Chilkoot, roads and railroads over White Pass. Some ideas materialized, most were merely dreams. Through it all, Dyea and Skagway competed to become the gateway to the North. On May 27, 1898, construction began on Alaska's first railroad and in less than a year it reached the summit of White Pass. Skagway — the most northerly port on the continent then connected with a railroad — emerged the clear winner, but by that time the gold rush was all but over.

Dyea did not die easily. From the start, the town's promoters worked hard to attract transportation companies interested in improving the Chilkoot trail. Minnesota engineer George Brackett, who ended up building the main wagon road out of Skagway, first thought Dyea was the place to be and bought land there. Even though railroad backers chose White Pass as the way to go, they looked again at Dyea when Skagway balked at meeting their demands.

During the early months of the rush, the trail advantage seesawed with the weather, and along each route men made spotty upgrades. Stampeders built log bridges over the worst muck-holes on the White Pass trail; over on the Chilkoot, several toll bridges went up across the Taiya River. The White Pass route became increasingly popular with pack trains during late fall as freezing temperatures hardened the trail, and in November 1897 Brackett started building his wagon road out of Skagway. Over on the Chilkoot, tramway construction began to compete with the White Pass trail for freight. Deep winter cold and frozen interior waterways forced many stampeders to bide their time in Skagway and Dyea. But in February 1898, traffic picked back up, beginning the biggest surge yet of gold-seekers. A log toll road for wagons opened from Dyea to Canyon City, and two entrepreneurs carved the Chilkoot's famous Golden Stairs in March, charging for their use until breakup.

By March, Brackett's road reached White Pass City, a trail town four miles below the summit. He had persevered in building his road despite a fraudulent survey, an unscrupulous associate and repeated money shortages. By April, four companies were hoisting buckets and sleds of freight on aerial tramways over Chilkoot Pass, and for a time Dyea gained bragging rights. In May 1898, after much lobbying by transportation developers eager to cash in on the gold rush, Congress finally okayed construction of toll roads and railroads in Alaska. Five companies — including

This second-hand Brooks 2-6-0 served as the White Pass and Yukon Route's first locomotive. (Courtesy of Nicki Nielsen)

FIRST LOCOMOTIVE IN ALASKA — SKAGWAY, JULY 20, 1898.

Getting clearance to lay tracks through Skagway was one of the railroad company's thorniest problems the first month of construction. The town granted a right-of-way along the bluff east of Spring Street, but did nothing to clear squatters from the property. Finally, in a stormy public meeting on June 15, 1898, that lasted until 3 a.m., the railroad was promised a temporary easement down Broadway Street. Downtown business owners protested and threatened to physically halt construction. But by the time they awoke later that morning, the Broadway track was practically in place. (Anchorage Museum, Photo no. B70.35.1)

Brackett's, albeit retroactively — applied to build from the coast to White Pass. Over in Canada, 21 companies were proposing railroads into Yukon Territory.

About this time, Canadian railroad contractor Michael J. Heney appeared in Skagway. Known as the "Irish Prince," he had worked nearly a decade for the Canadian Pacific Railway, and had surveyed CPR's line from interior British Columbia to the Pacific coast, through mountains and along rivers. Now he was anxious for a new project. He walked the White Pass trail to Lake Bennett, scribbling observations in his notebook. Despite the daunting terrain, he decided he could build a railroad through the mountains, if he could get financial backing. Tired and dirty from the 40-mile hike from Bennett back to Skagway, he checked into the St. James Hotel where he ran into three men with a similar agenda *and* the needed money. Surveyors Sir Thomas Tancred and John Hislop and engineer E.C. Hawkins were checking out possible railroad routes for the Close Brothers Co., a London-based investment bank. The Close Brothers had loaned money to the British syndicate that had financed Moore's early efforts and planned to build a railroad through White Pass. When the loan could not be repaid, the Close Brothers assumed control of the railroad project. Far into the night, the men talked through the haze of Havana cigars. By morning, Heney had accepted the job as general foreman for the White Pass and Yukon Route (WP and YR) railroad. Construction started the next month on a route that snaked above Brackett's wagon road.

Brackett's road continued to draw heavy pack-train traffic through fall 1898. Railroad company president Samuel H. Graves paid Brackett for damages caused by railroad construction. But the railroad needed to control all freighting to become profitable. Graves finally struck a deal to buy out Brackett. Meanwhile Brackett was having his own problems. The packers were having to drop their rates to compete with the railroad, and Brackett's tolls increasingly cut into their shrinking profit margins. In January 1899, a cattle driver refused to pay the toll and chopped down the gate at White Pass City. Other irate packers followed his example in what escalated into the Toll Gate War. By the time the dispute reached court, the railroad had reached the summit. The packers were out. The Brackett wagon road — Alaska's first improved road — saw limited use during the next several winters when snow blocked the railroad. It soon deteriorated into disuse.

About the White Pass and Yukon Route, historian Edwin Bearss wrote, "It is unlikely that there was ever a railroad built with so little advance planning. There had been only sketchy preliminary surveys, no rolling stock or construction materials had been assembled. It was hundreds of miles to the nearest base of supplies." Workers rarely numbered fewer than 1,000 and at times nearly 2,000 were on the payroll, working round-the-clock through summer. Construction camps popped up along the line, where the men were fed hearty, hot meals. Telephone lines connected the camps with headquarters in Skagway. The railroad provided steady work when prospecting did not, and workers came and went with rumors of gold strikes; more than 800 workmen deserted in August 1898 with news of gold at Atlin. Heney allowed no liquor in the camps; when one of Soapy's thugs tried to set up a drinking and gambling tent, Heney ordered an early morning blast that dropped a boulder on the tent and whiskey stocks, and sent the would-be bartender cursing down the mountain in his long johns.

Construction was a dangerous, expensive nightmare. Narrow-gauge tracks of only 36 inches reduced the road bed width, a concession to costs through the precipitous mountains. But local timber splintered, and Oregon lumber was shipped in. Almost every mile of roadbed required blasting of granite and quartzite, which took large amounts of dynamite and black powder. Crews often dangled on ropes from mountainsides as they worked. The railroad operated its own hospital. Thirty-five workers died on the grade, including Maurice Dunn and A. Jauxenu, crushed by a 100-ton granite rock at mile 11 as they drilled holes for blasting powder. The rock was too big to move, so they were left entombed. The stone was painted with a black cross and remains as a monument to those who died.

On July 21, 1898, the railroad ran its first excursion train to the construction front at

The White Pass and Yukon Route's first excursion train on July 21, 1898, carried about 150 passengers, including 22 tourists off the City of Seattle. They rode on two flatcars temporarily equipped with wooden benches for seats. Here the passenger train is shown crossing the second bridge over the Skagway River, although the photograph is incorrectly dated. The first work train carrying timbers and iron to the construction front ran on July 20, a day before the excursion train. (Courtesy of Nicki Nielsen)

This view looks south from a half-mile below the summit of White Pass. Brackett's wagon road snakes through the canyon to White Pass City, above which a pack train advances toward the summit. The railroad grade can be seen across along the upper left mountainside.
(Special Collections Division, University of Washington Libraries; E.A. Hegg photo #595)

Rocky Point. Guests dined on caviar and chutney. By August, work trains were running between Skagway and Heney Station at mile 12, and two freight and passenger trains a day commenced shortly after. Work continued steadily and slowly through winter. On Feb. 20, 1899, the first train to the summit arrived with two coach cars crowded with 100 guests. *The Skaguay News* proclaimed "We are 2,900 feet closer to Heaven." The men were treated to cigars and hard liquor in one tent; the women to sherry and a blazing heater in another. Then they were served a lavish dinner with caviar and champagne as temperatures outside dropped to 22 degrees below zero.

On July 6, 1899, the railroad reached Lake Bennett with much fanfare and champagne celebrating. The next year, on July 29, railroad crews working north from Bennett and south from Whitehorse met at Caribou Crossing (now Carcross) to drive the final golden spike. In the meantime, Dyea had withered to only a few residents, primarily teamsters and tramway operators who unsuccessfully sought to have their town made part of Canada. After the railroad reached Bennett, the tramways closed and were sold to the railroad.

The WP and YR succeeded in audacious engineering. The 110-mile line from Skagway to Whitehorse crossed wicked terrain, with 516 curves, 71 bridges and culverts and a 250-foot tunnel through a rock barrier. Near the summit, an awesome feat was accomplished in 1901 with construction of a steel cantilever bridge 215 feet above the stream bed of a yawning canyon. Before construction of the bridge, tracks ran along each side of the canyon, joined at the canyon's narrow end in a "Y" with a switch, a section of deadend track and a locomotive turntable; the engines were turned to face the right direction and the cars reattached so the train could continue through the switchback. During construction of the line, equipment and machinery frequently had to be pulled by hand up the mountainsides and rock faces. The railroad's first 21 miles in Alaska climbed 2,885 feet from sea level to the summit, which meant the engine was frequently 30 feet higher on the mountain than the caboose. The railroad cost $10,000 a mile for three flat miles in Skagway, to $125,000 a mile for the most expensive stretches at Tunnel Mountain and Rocky Point. The line stayed open in winter with rotary snow plows pushed through by two and three locomotives, with the train close behind. Once an avalanche swept a rotary off the tracks and down the mountain, injuring two of the three men on board.

The railroad ensured Skagway's permanency, even when the town's post-gold rush population dipped to several hundred. By 1904, almost 12,000 passengers were riding the railroad with more than 30,000 tons of freight carried annually.

Just as gold spurred its construction, ore from Canadian mines continued to be its primary freight. In the mid-1920s, the WP and YR began hauling lead, silver and zinc concentrates from the Yukon and crude copper from the Whitehorse area. In the mid-1930s, the company expanded into aviation, and hired noted bush pilot Vernon

Bookwalter away from Clyde Wann's Skagway Airlines. White Pass's airline business soon included prospectors, policemen, trappers, dog teams, mail, freight and tourists. The company's wide-ranging transportation network included steamboats from Whitehorse downriver to Dawson City; a hotel at Atlin; a two-mile rail line connecting Tagish and Atlin lakes; and excursions that ran 1917 to 1955 from Carcross to the garden resort at Ben-My-Chree, at the south end of West Taku Arm. In 1940, White Pass sold its aviation divisions to Yukon Southern Airways.

In 1942, the military descended on Skagway. The town and its port became an important staging area for construction supplies and troops headed into the interior to build the Alaska-Canada Highway and work on the Canada Oil (Canol) Pipeline. The 770th Railroad Operating Battalion took over the railroad. The Army added 26 new locomotives and 253 freight cars to the line's rolling stock. The special Army engines were nicknamed "Gypsy Rose Lees" because they were "stripped for action." Locomotive No. 195 is displayed today beside the city museum. This engine originally was slated for shipment to U.S. military in Iran, but for some unknown reason it arrived in Skagway. The locomotive was no match for the White Pass, however, and was rarely used.

At its peak, the railroad operating battalion had about 800 men, recruited from 17 major railroads in the United States. Their first winter was one of the fiercest on record, with temperatures dropping to 68 degrees below zero. The local railroaders doubted the battalion could operate the line. Perhaps the troops did too. Pvt. Howard Foley, from the Long Island Railroad in New York, remarked: "That line's too steep for a goat and too cold for a polar bear."

But Lt. Col. William P. Wilson, formerly superintendent of the Burlington's line through the Rocky Mountains in Colorado, was in charge. Under his command, the "toughest 110 miles of track in the world" increased its tonnage more than ten-fold. Before the war, 1938 to 1941, the line averaged 25,000 tons a year. But by 1943, the White Pass moved 281,962 tons, shoving through as many as 34 trains a day.

White Pass and Yukon Route excursions to the summit and to Fraser, B.C. are popular with cruise ship passengers. Trains pulled by steam engines meet passengers at each of the three cruise ship docks. Diesel locomotives replace the steam engines at the railroad shop two miles north of town for the pull up the mountains. This scene at the new Broadway Dock shows Mount Harding in the distance on the right. (Dedman's Photo Shop)

Icy rails caused frequent train derailments. One train derailed on the steel cantilever bridge. Another time, troops had to chip away some cliff so a bulky piece of machinery for the Canol refinery could go around a hairpin curve. On another tight curve, three flatcars loaded with pipe toppled down the mountainside. When trains stopped, their wheels froze to the trails. In winter, 20-foot snow drifts stopped traffic until the rotary plows opened the line; in spring and fall, stream washouts and rock slides caused delays. The winter of 1942 brought one of the longest blockades of the railroad in its history, shut down by snow for two weeks. Army fireman Walter F. "Bull" Durham once told about being trapped in a caboose during that shutdown. The snow outside was level with the top of the caboose, and wolves circled, sniffing at the cupola protruding from the snow. Durham and his companion lay on the floor in terror, afraid to do more than whisper; they knew that their supply box contained raw steaks, the scent of which they feared would drive the wolves to madness. All they had in defense was an ax.

On May 1, 1946, the Army's lease was up. The railroad — with worn-out equipment — reverted to civilian management. Gradually, new rolling stock came on line. By the mid-1950s, much of the railroad's business came from the United Keno Hill lead-zinc mines in the Yukon and the Cassiar, B.C. asbestos mines. The railroad also carried increasing

Oscar Selmer

By Su Rappleye

Editor's note: *Su Rappleye has lived in Skagway for about a year. She is a Public Broadcasting Service reporter, who came to town by way of Haines.*

Oscar Selmer's family came to Skagway from Norway. His uncle, Pete Lunde, arrived in 1897, and wrote Oscar's parents to come too. "They landed in Skagway with my oldest sister, Birdie — she was about 2 and my brother, Osbourne (Occie), a babe in arms — in 1905." At first, Oscar says, the young family lived in Bennett, where his father worked for the White Pass railroad. "My sister Virginia was next in line, and she just about got born in Bennett, but my mother wouldn't stand for it so they took a push car — a hand car — and they hand-carried all the way to Skagway so she could have my sister born here."

In 1908, the family moved to Skagway, where Oscar Sr. opened a barber shop, a trade he had learned in Norway.

"I couldn't have asked for a better place to live as far as I'm concerned; there's better places and worse places, but to me this is home. And there's been a Selmer living on this property ever since 1910. Dad got this building, the old homestead they call it. It was a house of ill-repute down there on Third or Fourth Avenue that he got cheap."

Oscar says there were eight in the family eventually, five boys and three girls, and "we never were bored because we knew that we had to create our own entertainment." One method was music. "We had quite an orchestra in our family. My dad was an excellent violinist. My brother Victor played the clarinet or saxophone. My sister Pauline played the saxophone. I played the trumpet; and my mother, she would tap her foot. We had wonderful times."

And, yes, there were some not so wonderful times, too. Oscar says when he was 7 he stole a candy bar from Harry Ask's store, but he got caught. "I was so nervous. I said to Harry, 'Are you going to tell my dad?' 'Well,' he says, 'I'll have to think about that.' He kept me in sweat. If he'd told dad, I'd have got a licking and it would have been done. But he never did tell dad. But every once in a while I'd go down there and he'd say, 'Have you been behaving yourself? Yep, OK, but remember if you don't....' He held that over my head."

Of the eight Selmer children, Oscar says all but two worked for the railroad. "Occie and I worked the longest; Occie worked about 42 years, and I worked 36."

Oscar started as a summer baggage man with White Pass while he was still in high school, and graduated up to brakeman. "Mainly we used boxcars in those days, and you had to get on top of those boxcars to put the hand brakes on. It was quite an interesting ride: 20 below or 40 below, wind, snow, sleet, and you're outside on top of the boxcar. And you had to do all the boxcars. You had to walk the top of the train from one end to the other, so it wasn't just a case of getting on one boxcar and then sitting down for the ride. If you were going towards the engine you could see where the curves were, but then you had to go back the other way to do your work and then you couldn't see where the turns were. A little more difficult, but what you did was when you came to a straight stretch you'd run like the devil on the top of those cars."

Oscar never fell off the boxcars, but he was flipped off a flatcar one time in a freak accident that broke his leg and crippled him enough to end his brakeman career and put him to work in the shops.

It also kept him out of the service during the war, but Oscar did his part by working in an Oregon shipyard from 1942 to 1946, his only years out of Skagway. When he returned, he went to work in the White Pass paint shop, and that's also when he met and married his first wife, Alice. "I met her the first of August, and we were married on Sept. 15th."

Oscar is a short man at about 5'5", but he has as many answers for that as he has for everything else. "Everybody asks me how'd you ever kiss your wife. Alice was pretty near 6 feet tall. Well, I had a kid programmed. He had a little wagon, so he brought that wagon in just as they said you can kiss the bride now, and I stood in the wagon and kissed her right straight on."

Alice and Oscar raised three children before she passed away. Oscar now has six grandchildren, and a second wife, Judy, who he married in 1979, a year after his retirement.

"Every day I worked, if as brakeman or in the paint shop, I enjoyed going to work. It was something different every day; it was not just sitting down and adding the same figures all the time. And the mountains, animals; it was a great life, it really was."

At 73, Oscar continues to keep busy and interested. In the summer he likes to fish; in the winter he reworks his father's photographs.

Pioneer Oscar Selmer spent most of his working years with the White Pass and Yukon Route railroad. Except for a four-year stint in the 1940s, Oscar has lived in Skagway all his life. (Harry M. Walker)

"He had a darkroom and his camera was a 122, that's a postcard size, and he took lots of negatives. Of course I didn't realize I was going to do photography work when he was still living, or I'd have chewed him out a little bit. He could have taken some more pictures of Broadway. He didn't take any of his barbershop side of the street so much as he did across the street, which was handier for him I suppose, but anyway he had lots of negatives of various parts of Skagway during the early days."

Oscar always has time for humor. He and Judy were found one time, measuring the valley from one side to the other with a yardstick, a feat he says he had performed before much earlier in his life. Shortly thereafter a newspaper article appeared, assuring Skagway residents that the measurements had matched, and that the mountains were not closing in on the town.

shipments of building materials going north.

During this time, the WP and YR helped pioneer containerized shipping — a cost-saving innovation where freight is loaded into a metal box at the point of origin and remains in the container through transshipment. In 1955, the company launched the first ship built from the keel up for containerization.

In October 1963, the railroad shut down for the first time in its history when Canadian officials suspended the line's operations after wage negotiations with the American Teamsters' Union at Skagway stalled. A strike was averted, however, and after three nervous weeks for Skagway residents, who depended on the railroad jobs, trains started running again.

In 1965, White Pass put into service a new ship built for larger containers and added a sister ship in 1968. A customized form of container transportation contributed to opening the Cyprus Anvil Mine in Yukon Territory — at the time one of the richest lead and zinc deposits in the world. To service the mine, the railroad company spent $30 million to update equipment and handling facilities. This included new ore concentrate storage and expanded loading docks at Skagway, custom-built diesel locomotives and new containers, and a 50-truck fleet to haul ore from the mine to the railroad terminal in Whitehorse.

The WP and YR enjoyed a short-lived boom during the late 1960s. The railroad transshipped an unprecedented tonnage of

This early color postcard shows the wooden trestle over Glacier Gorge which connected Tunnel Mountain's east portal with the track to Skagway. (Courtesy of Nicki Nielsen)

freight, its primary customers being the Cyprus Anvil mine and the Clinton Creek asbestos mine in Yukon Territory.

Although freight accounted for almost 90 percent of the railroad's business, the company began looking to growth in passenger service. The extension of regular state ferry service to Skagway in 1963 and the opening in 1977 of the Klondike Gold Rush National Historical Park brought more and more tourists to town, and the train got its share. But the completion in fall 1978 of the Klondike Highway 2 provided an alternate overland route between Skagway and the interior, and added to problems that the railroad was beginning to have.

Labor problems at the Canadian mines and plummeting mineral prices threatened continued freight shipments. The Clinton Creek mine closed, costing the railroad more than a million dollars in revenue in 1979 and bringing about layoffs in Skagway. At the same time, the railroad was having to offer more generous labor packages to compete with the high-paying construction jobs on the new trans-Alaska pipeline. All the time, upgrades to the Canadian road system allowed trucks to carry more weight and be increasingly more competitive with the railroad.

Talk of a natural gas pipeline from Alaska's North Slope through Canada in the early 1980s spurred the company to gear up for shipping construction materials. The company ordered four custom-built locomotives and tested shipments of 38-

Workmen blasted through 250 feet of granite to build the only tunnel on the line. Construction machinery and equipment had to be hauled along twisting trails from a base camp nearly 1,000 feet below. (Special Collections Division, University of Washington Libraries; E.A. Hegg photo #617)

inch pipe through the mountains. But the end was near for the railroad's freighting years. A temporary shutdown in summer 1982 of the Cyprus Anvil mine became permanent in a worldwide recession that depressed mineral prices. This, and the closure of the Whitehorse copper and Cassiar asbestos mines, brought the shutdown of the White Pass and Yukon Route Railroad.

The closure stunned Skagway. The railroad had been the town's primary employer for decades; since 1960, 60 percent to 75 percent of the town's jobs

A White Pass and Yukon Route passenger train passes Slippery Rock, a huge granite slab that challenged railroad builders in October 1898. Men worked suspended from ropes to drill and blast the grade. (Dedman's Photo Shop)

had been with the railroad. When the WP and YR stopped rolling in October 1982, nearly 190 people in town lost their jobs and some 500 employees company-wide were laidoff. During the resulting upheaval, someone penciled out numbers showing Skagway drew enough tourists to sustain a summer-only rail excursion business. Some ex-White Passers tried to lease the railroad. An investor from New York talked of a $35 million purchase price but was unable to put together financing. Then Whitehorse businessman Rolf Hougen entered the mix. In the early 1900s, his grandfather had walked the White Pass trail because he lacked money to buy a train ticket. Now, Hougen joked, he wanted to buy the White Pass as a kicker to the family story. He put together a group of notable northern businessmen. But a purchase price could not be reached and on Christmas Eve 1987, Hougen announced the end of negotiations. It was a dismal present for Skagway.

In the meantime, WP and YR executives decided to reopen the line. On May 12, 1988, with the Skagway High School band playing the *Star Spangled Banner* and the first cruise ship of the season docked nearby, chief operating officer Marvin Taylor cut a ribbon and his granddaughter Paula broke a bottle of champagne over steam engine 73. Then it chugged to the summit of White Pass with 250 passengers in the first train to roll in more than five years.

The summer excursions expanded with service to Fraser, B.C. in 1990, and in 1991 the railroad carried a record 100,000 passengers. The three-hour trip to the summit, at 1992 prices of $72 an adult and $36 a child, buys what the railroad bills "A trip through history you'll never forget." The company's attention to passenger comfort, with cars providing handicap access and swivel seats for all-around viewing, makes the WP and YR's old nickname — Wait Patiently and You'll Ride — a relic of the past, to be remembered along with the builders, the military and its freighting heyday.

Garden City of Alaska

By Frank Norris

Editor's note: *National Park Service historian Frank Norris was a seasonal historian and interpreter in Skagway from 1983 to 1988. While there, Norris was encouraged to write this article by Charlotte Jewell, local businesswoman and leader of the effort to revive the gardening culture for which the town had earlier been known. Ms. Jewell spearheaded a drive to earn $10,000 for mountain ash trees to line the road from the ferry terminal to downtown Skagway. Those who contributed $100 were recognized with a plaque at the base of one of the trees.*

Skagway exploded into prominence in July 1897 when news of the gold rush reached the outside world. Within months, thousands trooped north in search of fortune, and Skagway, at the foot of one of the most accessible passes between the civilized world and the gold fields, became indelibly stamped with the wild atmosphere that characterized the gold rush era.

Scarcely two decades later, the isolated town became almost as famous as a respectable place, all symbolized by its flower gardens. Half a century of Skagway tourists relished the products of the "Garden City of Alaska."

Miners Savor Fresh Produce

The oldtimers who populated the Yukon River settlements before the Klondike rush were a determined, hardy breed and carried abundant supplies. They knew the value of fresh produce for prevention of disease and for variety in an otherwise endless menu of beans, flapjacks and coffee. To meet that need, Dyea pioneers John J. Healy and Edgar Wilson in the 1880s and 1890s opened up a large garden behind their trading post. Many of the early prospectors purchased vegetables here before crossing into the Yukon frontier.

The news of Klondike gold ended the tranquility of the area surrounding Skagway and Dyea. Not surprisingly, the hectic atmosphere left little time for plant cultivation. Many of the stampeders cared little about gardening. Moreover, the area — and almost all of Alaska for that matter — was *terra incognita* regarding agriculture.

Early experiments showed, however, that proper care resulted in handsome yields. Sam Herron, who managed Healy and Wilson's trading post, routinely grew cabbage, lettuce, cauliflower, beets, peas, carrots, potatoes and parsnips, as well as flowers and hay. In Skagway, several families raised civic eyebrows with the abundance of their potato harvests. In October 1898, *The Skagway News* gushed that a six-hill patch near 14th and Main yielded an "average of 653 bushels to the acre, notwithstanding that the (McIntyre) family had removed the larger potatoes from the hills during the summer."

The most enthusiastic gardener was George Sexton. A graduate of Kansas State Agricultural

Growing vegetables was a necessity in pioneer days, but in later years the cultivation of flowers became increasingly important. Organized efforts to enhance the town's beauty lead to many gardens and flower-lined walkways. (Steve McCutcheon)

College, Sexton was the local agent for the U.S. agricultural station at Sitka. He planted a variety of vegetables, as well as oats, clover, barley and flax. He had success with carrots, cress, lettuce, mustard, onions, parsley, peas, radishes, rutabagas, rhubarb and salsify. He was particularly ecstatic about his turnips. "Alaska," he intoned, "appears to be the home of the turnip."

1898 proved critical for Skagway. As the gold rush ran its course, the railroad brought stability to the town. Churches, social clubs, schools, wives and other entrapments of civilization soon evolved, adding an air of permanence.

Farming Invades the Valleys

Gardens manifested this permanence. Emboldened by the successes of a few 1898 horticulturists, more residents planted vegetables and flowers the following year. Incipient gardeners soon recognized that Skagway had advantages lacking in other Southeast communities. The Skagway Valley had relatively low rainfall, thus lessening the leaching of nutrients from the soil. The area had a higher percentage of sunlight and longer summer days. Although not of uniform high quality, the soil in some areas, a residual forest loam, was excellent for growing crops and flowers.

The town's increased population encouraged the growth of several market gardens around the turn of the century. Most growers cultivated truck gardens, but some grew a variety of grains. These small farms produced primarily for the Skagway market, but on occasion distributed their products to Haines, Whitehorse or Juneau.

During the first two or three years of the 20th century, market farmers spread out into both the Dyea Valley and the northwestern end of Skagway Valley. The pioneering partnership of Henry E. Nicolai and Henry C. Clark tilled land in both places. Nicolai concentrated on Dyea, while Clark worked mostly on land across the Skagway River from the railroad shops. Many Skagway oldtimers fondly remember the Clark farm. His 40-acre tract was the largest in the valley. Among his specialties was rhubarb. His plants were so large and tasty that locals dubbed him the Rhubarb King.

Nicolai worked a portion of a 140-acre homestead in Dyea in the midst of the decaying gold rush town. He also started one of Skagway's first dairies in late 1899. Other early market gardeners were William H. Joy, A.H. Wild and H.N. Holmes. There also was a short-lived White Pass Farm just before World War I, which grew vegetables for the WP and YR's Yukon riverboat fleet.

The market gardeners' goal was to make Skagway self-sufficient in vegetables, milk, poultry and feed grain production. The first glimmer that such a goal was within reach was the *Daily Alaskan*'s prediction in April 1900 that "after a season or two, Skagway consumers of garden truck will be able to get a big share of such products from their own gardens and farms." The first known advertisements

In spring 1902 jeweler Herman Kirmse organized a gardening contest for Skagway. Kirmse promoted the town's gardens to such an extent that it was not long before the White Pass and Yukon Route used Skagway's gardens in its own advertisements. Herman Kirmse's children, Hazel (left) and Jack, continued their father's promotion of the town. They pose here outside their jewelry and curio shop with Lillian Black, wife of George Black. (Courtesy of Mrs. James Doogan)

for homegrown farm produce appeared that spring. Farmers had a good year and increased local production in 1901, diversifying into onions, beets, pumpkins and strawberries, and featuring door-to-door deliveries.

Few flower gardens existed before 1900, but a strong upsurge in floriculture appears to have taken place that year, followed by scores of new residents planting for the first time in 1901. U.S. agricultural agent C.C. Georgeson looked over the town's gardens during a stopover in 1901 and was astonished by Skagway's "carpet-like" lawns and flowered dooryards.

Pride in Flower Gardens

As popular as gardening had become, it was predictable that townspeople wanted to display their harvest. Recognizing the inherent advertising value of sending such products Outside, the Chamber of Commerce arranged to send a display of 12 varieties of hardier vegetables and examples of barley, wheat, rye and oats to the Portland Exposition in fall 1901. Most of the vegetables came from the garden of Charles O. Walker, the city's poundmaster at that time. Eight years later, flowers were sent to the Alaska-Yukon Pacific Exposition in Seattle.

To stimulate interest in local flowers, jeweler Herman Kirmse organized a citywide gardening contest in spring 1902. He formed a committee that in mid-August would tour the town's flower gardens and select prize winners. Kirmse himself presented

One of the best known gardens in the years between the world wars was that of Will and Ann Blanchard on Sixth Avenue. The garden featured carnations, gladiolus, asters and white lilacs, and was an important stop for tourists. (Courtesy of Mrs. James Doogan)

the unanimous first prize to Mrs. Marian Reynolds, who received a half dozen Rogers Brothers 1847 silver knives and forks. Second place winner, Mrs. Jeannette de Gruyter, was presented with a silver pickle castor.

Largely through Kirmse's efforts, the community was well aware of its flower gardens by 1905, and the White Pass and Yukon Route began to recognize the annual flower show as a resource. Gardens, particularly flower gardens, were a perfect way to publicize the civility of the community and to provide the contrast needed for railway advertising. Skagway offered gardens in abundance, and although gardens were plentiful in a few other northern communities, particularly Dawson City, Skagway had the advantage of being easily accessible. In addition, the town's location between train and ship gave visitors time to view local gardens.

As early as 1906, a White Pass pamphlet described the town as offering "a profusion of flowers, trim lawns and prolific gardens." Thereafter, most WP and YR promotional booklets presented garden photographs and information. Tourists enjoyed the contrast between the gardens and the frontier atmosphere. Local hotel owners, including George and Clara Dedman of the Golden North and Harriet Pullen of Pullen House, planted flowers on their properties.

The town's early gardeners were a cross section of the community. Perhaps 60 to 70 percent of the early gardeners were women, who focused on flowers. Men seemed to prefer vegetable gardens.

The homes of Skagway's early gardeners were spread throughout the valley. One of the better known gardeners was Mrs. E.J. Shaw, wife of an accountant on Moore's Wharf who lived near Fourth and State. Another was Mrs. Lee Guthrie, wife of a saloon owner, who lived at Eighth and Main and was admired for having "the most varied and most costly" flowers in Skagway, according to the *Daily Alaskan*. Perhaps the best known was Mrs. W. Lyle Speer, wife of a railroad baggageman and expressman, who lived at Eighth and Broadway. Mrs. Speer cultivated strawberries, grew the town's only rose bush — a pink double rose — and once harvested a 43-ounce head of lettuce.

"Garden City of Alaska"

Just before the United States entered World War I, tourism throughout Alaska surged. Dr. L.S. Keller, the local dentist and newspaper editor, reacted to the trend by creating the slogan "Skagway, Garden City of Alaska" and using it in various news stories. The slogan proved apt, and the city retained it in some form for almost 40 years.

Skagway citizens did what they could to help win the war. A few joined the military, but more assisted through local gardening. The cultivation of flowers gave way to vegetables. As the *Daily Alaskan* phrased the situation, "nearly all the available space in the yards and lawns was given over to raising things needful, and the plebeian potatoe (sic) took the place of the stately and aristocratic dahlia." Even isolated homesteads, such as the Dyea parcel of William E. Matthews, played a role. In July 1917, a group of prisoners used a portion of Matthews' land to plant 300 cabbage plants for a "loyalty garden."

After the war, flowers once again dominated local gardens. The interest in gardening remained as strong as ever, but the number of tourists began climbing to record levels. The number of train passengers increased from less than 2,500 in 1915 to 9,800 in 1927. Keller resurrected his prewar slogan in about

1919 and continued to use it for the remaining five years in which he published his newspaper.

Skagway's Gardening Heyday

Skagway's gardeners experimented with a diversity of flower varieties. The town's best known flowers of the period were dahlias, sweet peas, pansies and nasturtiums. Brochures gave seemingly unbelievable dimensions to Skagway's flowers. The dahlias, they said, were "ten inches in diameter," "as big as dinner plates," or "as big as your hat." Sweet peas were advertised as being nine feet high, "with stems a foot long and vines running up more than six feet." Pansies were "3 1/2 inches wide," or "as large as tea cups." Nasturtium vines reputedly grew three inches in 24 hours.

The best known local garden between World Wars I and II was that of Will and Ann Blanchard. In addition to the popular flowers, this garden featured carnations, gladiolus, asters and white lilacs. The Blanchards had been active in Skagway gardening shortly after the gold rush, and George Blanchard had been a judge for Kirmse's early contest. Will and Ann had lived on Sixth Avenue west of Main Street since 1906. Their garden was attracting notice even before World War I, and for 20 years after the war it was a "must see" stop for Skagway tourists.

The dahlia became the Blanchards' speciality. Much as fellow resident Fred Weber had done a decade before, the Blanchards experimented with many varieties. Ernest Hall noted 36 of them in a 1932 visit. The Blanchards' cultivation was so successful that a 1929 dahlia was advertised as the world's largest, a distinction held for more than 30 years.

Bachelor Charley Walker owned another well-known Skagway garden on Ninth Avenue. This pioneer worked many jobs around town; he was the one who had attached the 20,000 driftwood sticks onto the facade of the Arctic Brotherhood Hall. Walker often sold bouquets to disembarking tourists, and shipped flowers to customers in Juneau. He boasted one of the few greenhouses in town, and prided himself on being called "the most northern florist in the world," a distinction he felt he earned because he sold bedding plants and supplied flowers to the southbound Canadian Pacific Railroad ships. The Walker and Blanchard gardens were open to visitors when ships were in port, and Skagway's gardens were an important part of Martin Itjen's famed streetcar tours in the 1920s and 1930s.

World War II and its Aftermath

The image of Skagway as the "Garden City of Alaska" suffered a major jolt with the coming of World War II. In March 1942, the town received its first battalion of troops, who were put up in tents on the margins of the small airstrip. Throughout the next year, they were followed by thousands more. The soldiers came to run the railroad, to assist in the movement of goods needed to hack out the Alaska Highway and to construct the Canol oil pipeline from Skagway to Norman Wells in Canada's Northwest Territories. The Army commandeered almost every vacant lot in town and laid river rock over the topsoil to provide a stable foundation for buildings for its troops. Army bulldozers uprooted many of the mountain ash that had been so carefully planted just five years earlier.

The troops left Skagway in 1946, and before long the tourists returned. Many of the earlier gardeners had died or sold their land, but a new wave of horticulturists brought color to the town's neighborhoods.

Interest in Gardening Declines

Skagway continued to be an active gardening community through the 1950s. However, interest in gardening was beginning to wane. The decline was neither sharp nor particularly notable at the time, and took place primarily because many of Skagway's foremost gardeners retired and were not replaced by others. The tradition of family vegetable plots was fading; perhaps the more timely delivery of fresh vegetables from steamships discouraged the tillage of local plots. Whatever the reason, Skagway had a relatively small number of gardeners by the late 1960s.

Gardening languished through the early 1980s even though there still were some outstanding vegetable and flower plots. Edna Kalvick's Skagway garden was featured in *Sunset* magazine and, more than a decade later after she moved to Dyea, her thriving vegetable plots were pictured in *ALASKA GEOGRAPHIC*'s issue, *Alaska's Farms and Gardens*.

The Garden Club's Revival

In fall 1982, local businesswoman Charlotte Jewell suggested at a city council meeting that hanging flower baskets would enhance the beauty of the historic district. This suggestion led to the formation of the Skagway Garden Club in March 1983. Once organized, the club lost little time in organizing a series of ambitious projects. Its members planted flowers in tires in the harbor area, and planted a lawn and flower bed in the traffic island at the ferry terminal.

In May 1985, the club spearheaded a campaign to finance the planting of 50 mountain ash along the road leading to the ferry terminal. The trees were planted in June 1986, and in 1987 Mountain Ash Row was dedicated at the July 4th ceremony.

The revival of gardening in the 1980s was almost as dramatic as the initial surge in the aftermath of the gold rush. On Broadway, where once nary a flower could be seen, are now found scores of plantings. With impetus from the Skagway Garden Club, townspeople have revived their plots and done much to restore the community's reputation for beautiful gardens. So successful have been their efforts that in September 1988 former Gov. Steve Cowper officially proclaimed Skagway the "Garden City of Alaska."

After the Gold Rush

The gold rush, the railroad, Army troops during World War II, a natural deepwater port, a national historical park — all of these help make Skagway what it is today. And more and more, Skagway today is a place popular with tourists. In 1991, more than 315,000 people visited town. Its long-standing affair with tourism is reaching new heights.

Skagway's importance as a transportation center is unquestioned. Tourism is part of this. So is freight. As a link between the coast and the interior, people and goods flow in and out. Skagway's harbor has more docking space than any port in Alaska, and can accommodate up to five large cruise ships plus assorted smaller vessels at a time. Freight and petroleum arrive by barge or containership to be trucked or pumped through a pipeline into Canada. Trucks pass through town several times an hour with Canadian lead and zinc ore for shipment to smelters in Europe and Asia. The freighting business is more gritty and less glamorous than tourism and at times its compatibility with tourism has been debated, but it provides several dozen year-round jobs, prized commodities in an otherwise seasonal economy.

For years, Skagway was little more than a railroad town. Its economy depended almost entirely on the White Pass and Yukon Route, with its fuel barge operation, containership line, docks, railroad and — for a time — airline. Freight shipments constituted the railroad's primary business. Its passenger service, however, helped make Skagway a tourist destination. Most early promotional efforts came through the railroad's corporate advertising.

Tourism ebbed and flowed through the years, and by the late 1970s grew to the point where it provided Skagway a dependable summertime economy. In 1977, the National Park Service came to town to operate the newly created Klondike Gold Rush National Historical Park. More shops opened with an influx of artists and entrepreneurs who saw untapped opportunity in Skagway's growing appeal to visitors.

Then in 1982 the railroad shut down. About 190 people in town lost their jobs. A single opening with the city drew 30 applicants; another with the postal service drew 40. Families moved away. Without the railroad, tourism was about the only industry left. The townspeople — collectively and individually — acted to make the most of it. The city created a Convention and Visitor's Bureau and hired a tourism director. The downtown began

This July 1991 view looks north up Broadway and the historic district toward the head of Skagway Valley. The red building in the lower right corner is the restored White Pass and Yukon Route Depot that now houses the National Park Service visitor center. State Street is immediately west of Broadway, and the Skagway River flows on the west edge of town. (Dedman's Photo Shop)

Bob Rapuzzi

By Su Rappleye

At 71, Bob Rapuzzi is a busy man with a list of things to do and not a lot of time to sit about and gab; yet he is full of information and when questioned he can rattle it off quickly. "The Rapuzzi family has five generations from Skagway, and we've worked on the railroad for 113 years; plus I worked on the Alcan Highway, trapped, prospected, . . . and I have four journeyman trades."

Bob's grandparents, Teresa and Joseph, migrated from the Swiss border of northern Italy across the American continent to the West Coast, where they homesteaded 160 acres of grazing land on the Seattle waterfront. But Bob says his grandfather could not speak English well, and lawyers took the land away from him because he had not known anything about the taxes.

In 1897, the elder Rapuzzis moved to Skagway and opened the Washington Fruit Store, where they sold fruit and merchandise to the prospectors and miners headed into the Yukon for the gold rush. "Grandma, she was a wonderful woman, worked from early morning until late at night, and raised six kids in that store; had a big taffy hook on the wall, made her own taffy, and sold it in the front of the store. She gave more away then she ever sold, but they made a living.

Bob's father, Charlie, was an engineer for the White Pass and Yukon Route for 53 years, including on the train that carried the Queen of England, which he counted as the highlight of his career. Bob's son, Rick, worked as conductor and brakeman until the WP closed down its year-round work, and he is continuing the tradition by adding more years for the Alaska Railroad. In between the two, Bob himself put in 50 years for WP as a longshoreman, operating heavy equipment on the waterfront.

But Bob has lots of other stories to tell. "I started trapping mink and marten when I was 13. I had my own trap line, and I'll tell you what I did with the skins. I sold them to Sears & Roebuck, and they in turn gave me clothes. When I was 16, I worked construction for the road commission, when they were first building the road to Dyea. At 19 I was over in Pearl Harbor, welding for the Navy in a civil service job. Actually I got out of there 30 day before the Japanese hit."

Next Bob put three years into building the Alcan Highway. "I was a Signal Corp operator with the 93rd Engineers. [It was] 72 below and we were living in tents, and it was so cold we had to work in pairs and watch each other because your face would freeze. It'd turn white right away, so it was terrible. We had to get the truckers that came in off the road. They had hobnailed shoes on yet. They didn't have the packs and things that they needed for winter, cause they hadn't been shipped yet. The shoes froze to the steel deck, and they couldn't get their feet out. Lot of those fellows lost their toes, lost their heels. And when they got to our base camp, we had to cut their shoes off to get them out of the trucks."

Bob Rapuzzi also recalls working on the Klondike Highway 2, but not for pay. "The longshoreman all got together — about 30 or 35 of them — and went up there and brushed it out all the way from down below up to Black Lake, all free labor, to get it started. . . . We didn't get much backing — somebody might not like to hear this — but it was because WP was bucking it. They didn't want competition with their railroad. We were working for WP, and if they'd got mad at us, they might have done us out of a job, but they didn't."

A ham radio operator, Bob talks to people all over the world, and he remembers helping the community get information after the big earthquake of 1964. "All the lines were down, but people in town had relatives over there, and they'd come to me. I'd taken my rig down to rework it and I didn't have an antenna up, so I took out a coil of wire and threw it up on a tree. I was working the states and working Anchorage to find out about these people, if their cousins or their husbands or their sons or brothers were all right. I'd work all day and then I'd come home and people would want me to do this during the night, but I was young then and I could take it without sleep."

Bob says he wanted to know a little about everything, so he got his training through technical schools in winter, and it was through his trips to Seattle that he met Ivadell, his wife of 40 years. They met at the ice rink. "This other kid and I, we played a lot of hockey and we were going a little faster than we should have and I knocked her down on the ice. I bent down and picked her up and stood her back on her feet and that's how we got acquainted. Two years later we got married, and I brought her up to this country. She didn't know if she was going to like it; and it took about 11 years before she finally settled down to it, but now she's into everything." Says Ivadell: "He told me if I'd marry him I'd never have a dull moment, and I haven't." Bob chuckles: "That's pretty good that she'll admit it."

"We've had a good, happy life," he says as he pulls on his coat, anxious to be off getting things done before they leave on their annual trek to see their two kids and five grandchildren, and then spend the winter months in warm sunshine. "We've been everywhere and we've done a little bit of everything. And I love it here. Let's face it. In the summertime I can go out there and go fishing for halibut and get crab, and go over to my cabin, a 5-acre homestead at Soldier's Landing in Dyea Bay, and you can't beat that open life."

LEFT: *McCabe College, a Methodist college headed by Dr. Lamont Gordon, operated only two terms before it was sold to the federal government. Federal district court was held in the building until the 1950s. It now houses the Trail of '98 Museum and City Hall. When built in 1899, it was Alaska's first college and its first granite building.* (Steve McCutcheon)

BELOW: *Skagway's many visitor attractions include "Madam Jan's Gold Panning Camp." Here burley Buckwheat takes a break from reciting Robert Service poetry to place a garter on a visitor's leg, with the help of a modern-day dance hall girl.* (Harry M. Walker)

to get a face-lift. The park service began work on some of its historic buildings, including restoration of the train depot. Individuals got grants to restore privately owned structures, and the city began working on the boardwalks. Cruise ships continued docking in Skagway, with overland connec-tions provided via the 99-mile Klondike Highway 2. In a matter of five years, Skagway became the most desirable port destination in southeastern Alaska, according to surveys of cruise ship passengers. The number of visitors steadily increased and in 1988, the booming tourism industry brought the railroad back to Skagway as a summer-only passenger operation.

Picturesque and compact, Skagway

Skagway celebrates July 4th with banners, flags and a big parade through town. (Harry M. Walker)

today offers something for history buffs, sightseeing enthusiasts, shoppers and hikers. Surrounded by stunning scenery, Skagway is a bit of small-town America flaunting an outrageous past as one of the most visited places in Alaska.

Modern Tourist Destination

Skagway becomes a circus in summer. Thousands of tourists pack the streets May

Barbara Dedman Kalen

By Su Rappleye

Barbara Dedman Kalen has spent all but two of her 67 years in Skagway. She says growing up here was great. "Kids could play anywhere. We went all over, and our parents didn't have to worry about us. If we'd be wandering around and it looked like it was dinner time or something, the nearest grown-up would say, 'I think I hear your mother calling,' and if we did something that we shouldn't, the nearest grown-up would upend you and give you a slap. The whole town raised the kids. I think it was kind of nice."

Barbara also remembers the war years with a smile: "I was 17, and it was a wonderful time because there were all these young men in town. All the girls really had a blast cause there were so many guys. All of my classmates, we nearly all married servicemen during the war. We were the age to get married and, practically all of the young men were in one of the armed forces, so it was just kind of natural that that's the way it happened. I was 19 when I got married."

Barb married Edward J. Kalen — "Nobody called him Ed, they called him Kal," she says — and together they raised four children, who have provided her with five grandchildren and one great-grandchild.

Barb did her best to share her interests with her children, especially her love of theater, music and the out-of-doors. "I used to go to Upper Dewey Lake (elevation 3,000 feet) every summer with my kids, and we'd camp in the cabin up there. Inez Knorr used to go with her kids too, and we had sleeping bags that we just left up there. We'd carry a needle and thread and some wool patch material, and we'd spend an hour or so patching the sleeping bags, but it sure beat packing them up and down. I think for most of the kids that grew up in Skagway in my time, Upper Lake is what they get homesick for." One year Barb surprised family members and friends with T-shirts and jackets for Christmas that were printed with a design for the Upper Dewey Lake Swim Club. "It's a very informal organization that consists of people who have actually hiked to Upper Lake, not helicoptered, hiked, and gone in that water and swam. It's a very select organization, and if you've ever done it you're a member."

Barb still takes occasional treks to Upper Lake. "It's pretty much straight up and takes two to four hours depending on your age and condition, and how much you're carrying," she says. She also continues to spend her winters crosscountry skiing, including participating in the 10K Buckwheat Ski Classic. "I used to pack my skis to Lower Lake and ski around, or go up to White Pass summit and ski between trains, catching the afternoon train back."

Barb is still active as a photographer. She says she's been taking pictures all her life. "My mother turned me loose with a camera, so I took pictures when I was a kid." Barb's parents started Dedman's Photo Shop, which Barb owns and operates now as the oldest family business in Skagway.

"We did picture finishing. Mother would have the news agents collect the pictures. It was all black-and-white roll film, and we'd run down to the boat, and get the [film], and come back and develop it, and then my mother would print them. When I was big enough, I got to take the pictures down to the ship and collect the money. I was 12 or 13 by the time I was trusted to go down and do that."

"And the folks always took pictures of things that went on in Skagway. We've got boxes and boxes of Skagway history. Mother started collecting and copying early day photos, the gold rush stuff, so we have a pretty fair library of early day photos that are in the public domain now."

But Barb says the photos she inherited from her parents were never cataloged, a frustration that taught her to label and date her own. "There was one particular argument about when the bridge was built, the highway bridge. I found a picture of it, sometime in the 1920s I think, and all the envelope said was 'New Bridge.' They should never have been that careless with the stuff. So now I really think that somebody else could come along and dig through my pictures and know what they were looking at."

Barb says she didn't work steady when she was raising kids, other than to take care of the slide business at the photo store, and in the early 1960s when she worked for two to three years at the post office. But she admits to being Skagway's reporter. "As secretary of the Chamber of Commerce, I was asked to write a piece about Skagway for newspapers. It turned into a bush column for the *Fairbanks News Miner*, the *Juneau Empire* and the *Whitehorse Star*. I wrote it as a letter to friends and got 10 to 15 cents an inch, plus $5 for pictures. I had to write for all three papers to break even, and ended up a newspaper correspondent for 20 years."

Barb says her Grandpa Dedman came for the gold rush in spring 1898, and he started out pretty penniless. "He did laundry for a few weeks, then eased himself into the hotel business." Barb's grandfather first owned the 4th Avenue Hotel, but bought a building he called the Golden North Hotel, and moved it from State and Second to Broadway and Third. Barb says this was the largest building in town that was ever moved. Barb says the building was not even a hotel at the time, and that later owners claimed a ghost story was connected with it. In fact, she says they "borrowed my daughter's wedding dress and had a photographer take a picture of the ghost, then they airbrushed the girl out so they only had a picture of the wedding dress."

Of living in Skagway, Barb says: "I like Skagway; it's a comfortable town and it's home. I've got a business that supports me, raised my kids here, and I have friends here. It's nice to go out; it's nice to visit elsewhere. It's nice to go to plays and concerts, but it's nice to come home and get out of the traffic. I enjoy getting away for a little while, but I enjoy coming home too. Folks in Skagway — and I'm not the only one — we've got roots here, we know who we are, where our family has been."

Barbara Dedman Kalen, granddaughter of gold rush pioneers, has lived in Skagway most of her life. (Courtesy of Barbara Dedman Kalen)

through August. Cruise ships out of Vancouver converge in Skagway's harbor on Tuesdays and Wednesdays, and the town of 700 swells with nearly 8,000 people. At its busiest, Skagway resembles gold rush boom days when the population rocketed to 10,000 people. "Days like those, we are extremely challenged," says the city's tourism director Jerre O'Farrell Fuqua.

Skiers enjoy a sunny February day at White Pass. (Dedman's Photo Shop)

FACING PAGE: *A thick blanket of snow covers the Case-Mulvihill House, built in 1904 for W.H. Case, a partner in the Case and Draper photographic firm. W.J. Mulvihill, the chief dispatcher for the White Pass and Yukon Route, lived here with his family from about 1914 until 1949. Although Skagway gets less precipitation than some other areas of southeastern Alaska, the town still receives about 35 feet of snow annually. Temperatures range from an average of 24 degrees in January to 57 degrees in July.* (Harry M. Walker)

The townspeople work, work, work through summer. They open their shops early and close late at night. For most Skagway residents, summer's income pays winter's bills. In 1991, the town's visitors brought in about $20 million.

Once the tourist season ends, business slows considerably. Summer employees leave. Half of the town's hotels, including the 209-room Westmark Inn, close. Many downtown shops are boarded up for the winter, nailed shut with panels painted to meet city code, to keep the place from looking neglected. A few stores stay open through the winter, to serve the folks who live in Skagway year-round and the few winter tourists. Its population is predominantly white and middle-class. Skagway is not a traditional Indian village, and its Native community is small and dispersed. The 20 or so Tlingits who live in Skagway belong to Sealaska Corp., the regional Native corporation headquartered in Juneau, and are represented locally by the low-profile Skagway Traditional Village Council.

For Skagway's permanent residents — many of them third and fourth generation gold rush and railroading families — winter is a time to regroup. To visit. To skate and ski. To cheer on the high school basketball Panthers. To catch up on things undone through the summer. Skagway loves the tourists, for without them it would be practically nothing. But hosting a four-month stream of visitors is wearing. Busy shop owners find themselves cooped behind counters on pretty summer days when they would rather be puttering in their gardens or hiking nearby trails. Winter also offers respite from the barrage of questions asked by tourists fresh off the boats: How far above sea level is Skagway? What lake is it on?

RIGHT: *A work crew at Lower Dewey Lake in 1906 takes a break from clearing a place to build a cabin. The man pulling the string is Bill Feero. To his right is Guy Sipprell; behind Bill is Nick Hansen and to Nick's left in the shadow of the tree is Billy Wright. The other workers are unidentified.* (Courtesy of Mrs. James Doogan)

Skagway Attractions

Skagway's gold rush and railroading history feeds today's tourism. The town works hard to keep the look and feel of a place from a by-gone era.

Restoration of gold-rush-era buildings is ongoing by the National Park Service, the city and private individuals. Modern businesses operate out of a number of them. Dedman's Photo Shop is located in the original E.A. Hegg photographic studio. The Golden North Hotel features rooms decorated in antiques and named after gold rush pioneers. The Red Onion Saloon, a brothel during the gold rush, is today a favorite watering hole. The Trail of '98 Museum and the city's offices are located in the state's first granite building, built by the Methodists to house McCabe College. Park service architectural historian Robert Spude

As Skagway matured after the gold rush and construction of the railroad, some of the refinements of modern society became available to town residents. Local musicians, such as Frank Feero (third from left in back row) and George Black (fourth from left in second row), could join the cornet band. For those who preferred outdoor sports, there were tennis tournaments on planked courts, such as the one shown on the facing page, held July 3, 1915. (Above, courtesy of Mrs. James Doogan; facing page, Anchorage Museum, Photo no. B88.3.59)

presents a thorough discussion of Skagway's unique buildings in *Skagway, District of Alaska, 1884-1912* (1983).

Visitor entertainment abounds. There are variety shows, melodramas, walking tours, tours in vintage cars. A three-hour excursion by rail takes visitors up to the summit of White Pass, a breathtaking trip into the mountains. Flight-seeing tours in airplanes and helicopters out of tiny Skagway International Airport take visitors southwest over Glacier Bay or north of town to land on West Creek glacier, a feeder of the Chilkat Glacier. There is shopping galore. Summer brings artists of all descriptions to work in studios along Broadway. Historic buildings house gift shops, restaurants, bars and hotels.

Numerous hiking trails begin in Skagway. A mile-long stroll that crosses a footbridge over the Skagway River leads to picnic sites at Yakutania Point and Smuggler's Cove northwest of town. A longer jaunt goes to the Gold Rush Cemetery, where Soapy Smith and Frank Reid are buried. The city maintains trails to the reservoir and Lower Dewey Lake, located on a quarter-mile-wide bench about 500 feet above town. More strenuous hikes continue to Upper Dewey Lake, Devil's Punch Bowl and Sturgill's Landing (Magic Forest), or the trail to A.B. Mountain on the west side of the valley. And for the well-equipped and experienced backpackers, the ultimate challenge out of Skagway is the historic Chilkoot trail.

Among the first places where visitors to Skagway should stop are the city's information center in the Arctic Brotherhood Hall and the National Park Service visitor center in the restored train depot. They are located on lower Broadway. The Arctic Brotherhood, covered with some 20,000 pieces of driftwood, is possibly the most unusual building in Alaska. The building was home to a secret fraternal organization founded during the gold rush that at its height had 30 chapters. President Warren Harding was the Brotherhood's last inductee during his visit to Skagway in 1923.

Although the original Arctic Brotherhood ceased operating decades ago, membership is again awarded today to visitors who go on the city tour offered by the Skagway Street Car Co. Today's version of this historic tour occurs in a fleet of 1920- and 1930-era cars driven by costumed conductors. Martin Itjen ran the original Skagway Street Car Co. until his death in 1942. Much of his estate went to Skagway pioneer, the late George Rapuzzi, who brought out Itjen's street car for parades. Skagway businessman Steve Hites resurrected the company and tour in 1986.

A long-running tourist attraction is the "Days of '98" show. The show was started

some 65 years ago by Rapuzzi to help raise money for the hockey team. Pictures of some of the show's first dance-hall girls — now some of the town's older matrons — hang in the Eagles Hall, where the show is held. Through the years, the show has taken on a professional polish and now supports two casts with nightly shows. Co-producer Jim Richards all but becomes Soapy Smith in costume and character and strolls through town between performances.

Each year, Skagway celebrates the Fourth of July in fine style. Shops close — not an easy thing to do in the face of customers. A parade stretches down Broadway, circles the town's only bank, and doubles back. Notable past attractions include the

irreverent antics of the Bigger Hammer Marching Band, whose kazoo music was described as "skunk rock" by writer Ken Kesey, when he visited Skagway in 1982 during the filming of "Never Cry Wolf." The Bigger Hammer band formed in 1980, a spin off of the Bigger Hammer Construction Co., so named because "everyone always needed a bigger hammer," according to co-organizer Doug Sanvik, who later moved to Juneau.

Tent City with its show, "Madam Jan's Gold Panning Camp" plays daily in an old gold rush camp known as Liarsville, three miles north of town. Liarsville was so named because journalists camped here to interview stampeders on the White Pass trail. They reported stories of all kinds, including some greatly embellished ones. During World War II, Liarsville was the site of an Army hospital; after the war, it served a short time as the main tuberculosis sanatorium for southeastern Alaska. Today, however, visitors are treated to a gold rush experience in a recreated tent city by a beautiful waterfall. They pan for gold in sluice boxes salted to guarantee a find for everyone. A big fellow with a big beard named Buckwheat recites Robert Service poetry while his companion, a 200-pound McKenzie River husky, pants nearby. Gold rush ladies from the Red Onion tells stories from Skagway's days as a bordello town.

FACING PAGE: *Martin Itjen could easily be called "Father of Alaska Tourism." His hugely popular Skagway Street Car Co. offered 50-cent tours of Skagway, its historic gold rush buildings, its beautiful gardens and Soapy Smith's parlor, which he operated as a museum. Itjen charmed visitors. He described the sites in his thick Austrian accent and recited original "intentionally horrible" poetry. His 30-passenger street cars were customized buses that sported mechanical figures, such as a stuffed bear that waved and a life-sized mannequin of Soapy Smith. Itjen is shown here with a group beside one of his street cars at the harbor. He once said, "All the folks here work for the railroad except me, and I work for the tourists." (Courtesy of Mrs. James Doogan)*

In 1935, Martin Itjen loaded his street car on a steamship and headed to Hollywood to visit Mae West, who was getting box office raves for her newest movie, "Klondike Kate." They went out to dinner and posed together by Itjen's street car. Entertainment writers made much about "Klondike stampeder dates movie queen." In a classic exchange, Mae told Itjen, "You're awfully cute. I think I'll keep you here in Hollywood." Itjen replied, "Mae, you asked me to live in Hollywood for the rest of my sweet life, but I cannot leave old Skagway, my home, my heart, my wife. (Courtesy of Mrs. James Doogan)

Tourists Find Skagway

Skagway's gold rush days found a few tourists peppered among the thousands of stampeders. By 1900, the Klondike rush was over. But not Skagway's vitality, nor its appeal to visitors.

By the turn of the century only 3,000 people lived in Skagway, compared to its gold rush peak of 10,000. Yet the community forged ahead. In 1899, the Skagway Convention sent a representative to the nation's capital to request territorial status or some form of representation in Congress. In 1900, Skagway became Alaska's first incorporated town.

The new railroad and its sternwheel steamboat line found business with communities along the Yukon River, former gold rush camps grown into permanent towns needing food, clothing, and other supplies, as well as transportation in and out. The railroad carried a growing number of tourists, who came up the Inside Passage. They transferred at Skagway to the train and continued their trip inland to such places as Lake Bennett, Whitehorse and Atlin.

Beginning about 1914, tourism increased to Alaska. The formerly popular Grand

FACING PAGE: *Members of the Skagway Ladies' Aid Society pose for a photograph around 1920. Mrs. Zinken, wife of the Presbyterian pastor, stands on the far right. Seated second from right in front is Jenny Olson Rasmuson. Jenny and her husband Edward Anton Rasmuson met in Yakutat in 1904, where they were working as Swedish missionaries. During their seven years there, their children, Maude Evangeline and Elmer Edwin, were born. They then went to Minnesota for a few years, where Edward became a lawyer. In 1915, they returned to Alaska and the next year, he was appointed U.S. commissioner and deputy clerk of the district court in Skagway. Commissioners then were allowed to have a private practice, and Rasmuson became counsel for the newly opened Bank of Alaska, which was based in Skagway. In 1919, Rasmuson became the bank's president, the first of three generations of Rasmusons to direct growth of the bank, which became the National Bank of Alaska. Edward served as Skagway's mayor several terms.* (Courtesy of Mrs. James Doogan)

Tour of Europe became less popular as war talk escalated, and Americans began looking closer to home for adventure. In 1915, tourists riding the White Pass and Yukon Route totalled less than 2,500; by 1927, the number had increased to more than 9,800. By 1920, Skagway was an extended port stay for Canadian-based steamships that remained in town up to 36 hours.

During this time, Skagway was settling into a relatively mild mannered community. In October 1911, Skagway launched a car race to Whitehorse over the railroad tracks. Dr. Charles G. Percival and George D. Brown won the race in an Abbott Detroit Bulldog. The Women's Club was active and opened a library.

Too, the temperance movement found Skagway, beginning a campaign that brought prohibition to the territory. Even though Evangeline Booth had held temperance revival meetings in Skagway in 1898, the movement really took hold in 1915 when the first territorial convention of the Women's Christian Temperance Union was held in town, brought there by Skagway resident Mrs. S.E. Shorthill, who was Alaska's representative to the WCTU. The three-day session opened with a parade of Sunday School children carrying flags and singing temperance songs. Although Skagway residents voted to allow drinking in the local option election a few days later, the townspeople later voted "dry" in the 1916 election that brought prohibition to Alaska.

Skagway, as a departure point for folks from the interior to Outside, saw off the *Princess Sophia* on her final voyage to Vancouver in 1918. Only hours out of Skagway, she wrecked in a storm on Vanderbilt Reef in Lynn Canal. All 353 passengers perished, a loss of many people from the Yukon and Alaska. Skagway native Hal Johnston Jr. said his father, an agent for the Canadian Princess ships, had to go to Juneau to identify the bodies. The tragedy brought about redesign of life preservers, he said.

As travelers continued coming through Skagway, a grassroots visitors bureau developed. The stampeders had been touched by gold, and their stories enchanted the tourists. Early on, there were flamboyant figures like Frank Keelar, the self-declared "Money King of Alaska" who made deals large and small. Pioneer businessman and jeweler Herman Kirmse became world renowned for his creations in gold, gold nuggets, Alaska ivory and silver. In 1898, he had made a three-pound watch chain out of gold nuggets won by Skagway gambler Pat Renwick, and after Renwick's death in 1906 the chain was displayed at Kirmse's store. In later years, the shop was operated by Herman's son, Jack.

In 1908, Peter Kern, another Skagway jeweler, built Alaska's first resort. Kern's Castle, as it was known, was a three-story Swiss-type chalet on a steep trail above Lower Dewey Lake. Visitors hiked 40 minutes, about 1,250 feet up the hillside to the hotel for refreshments, meals, overnight lodging, and a fine view of the town below. Kern hired a Mr. Sengfelter to paint a 50-foot watch on a cliff above town as advertisement; in the 1960s, the watch was repainted, the cost underwritten by Jack Kirmse, and the message changed to say "Kirmse's Curios." In July 1912, the castle burned in a forest fire.

Harriet "Ma" Pullen and her Pullen House Hotel were among Skagway's most famous attractions for a number of years. The gold rush had provided opportunities for a number of women spunky enough to meet the challenge, but few succeeded as completely as did Harriet Pullen. She

Even after the gold rush, Skagway remained a frontier town with occasional crimes and misdemeanors. On Sept. 15, 1902, an unidentified man tried to rob the Skagway branch of the Canadian Bank of Commerce. Waving a revolver in one hand and some sticks of dynamite in the other, the robber demanded $20,000. An unsuspecting lawyer, John G. Price, entered to make a deposit, and the startled robber fired his gun, setting off the dynamite. The explosion wrecked the bank, sending $2,800 in gold dust into the air, blowing clerk George Wallace out the back door, and injuring another clerk Charles R.W. Pooley. The robber died a few hours later in the railroad hospital. The gold dust was recovered after the ruins were hosed down and the dirt around the bank run through a sluice box in the river. The robber merited less attention. His remains were sacked and stowed in a woodshed. They were later found and cremated, except for the skull. It wound up in Martin Itjen's museum on display until 1926, when the museum closed. (Courtesy of Mrs. James Doogan)

started selling homemade apple pies from a tent restaurant along the White Pass trail, then operated a pack train once her horses arrived from Washington, and finally opened a boarding house in a building rented from Captain Moore. She later purchased the building and opened the Pullen House Hotel, which was one of Alaska's finest hotels during its peak. Fresh produce and dairy products were among its trademarks, the food raised for a few years on Mrs. Pullen's farm in Dyea. In her later years, Mrs. Pullen told her story often, casting herself as a widow with three sons who found success through hard work. Some oldtimers say she came to Skagway with a husband, whom she later sent away. In any case, Mrs. Pullen knew how to enchant visitors and often met tourist ships at the dock. One of her most spellbinding stories, albeit embellished through the years, was her eyewitness account of Soapy Smith's shooting. Mrs. Pullen died in 1947, at age 86. Her hotel fell into disrepair and was torn down several years ago.

Of Skagway's promoters, though, Marten Itjen may have been the best. He had prospected in the Klondike, worked for a while as an undertaker (although Skagway, he said, was too healthy for the business) and ran the town's only Ford car dealership among various other enterprises. His relaxed manner and funny stories made him popular with visitors as early as 1915, when he drove a hack. In 1923, he met President Warren Harding's entourage at the docks with his combination hack and coal wagon cleaned to a luster and sporting new bench seats in the back. His taxi

Red Cross training played an important role in Skagway's preparation for World War I. From left are Mrs. McCann, Edna Feero, Mrs. Dorn (seated), Mrs. Blenda Goding, Myrtle Keller bandaging the head of Mrs. Ungerforn, nurse, Abby Sparks, Edith Feero Larson (seated), Ethel Feero Hansen, Agnes Schlosser (measuring medicine), Mrs. Van de Wahl, Mrs. Lena Hanson, Mrs Guyer and Emma Feero, widow of John Feero. (Courtesy of Mrs. James Doogan)

business grew into the original Skagway Street Car Co.

When Skagway's tourism collapsed in the depression of the 1930s, Itjen launched a one-man campaign to bring the visitors back. He took his street car to Hollywood and enjoyed a much-publicized date with movie star Mae West. For the next three weeks, he played a one-man Skagway show at the Orpheum in San Francisco and at another theater in Los Angeles. The next year in Skagway, tourism doubled.

World War II: Tourism Dies, Troops Arrive

Everything changed with the bombing of Pearl Harbor and the United States' entry into World War II.

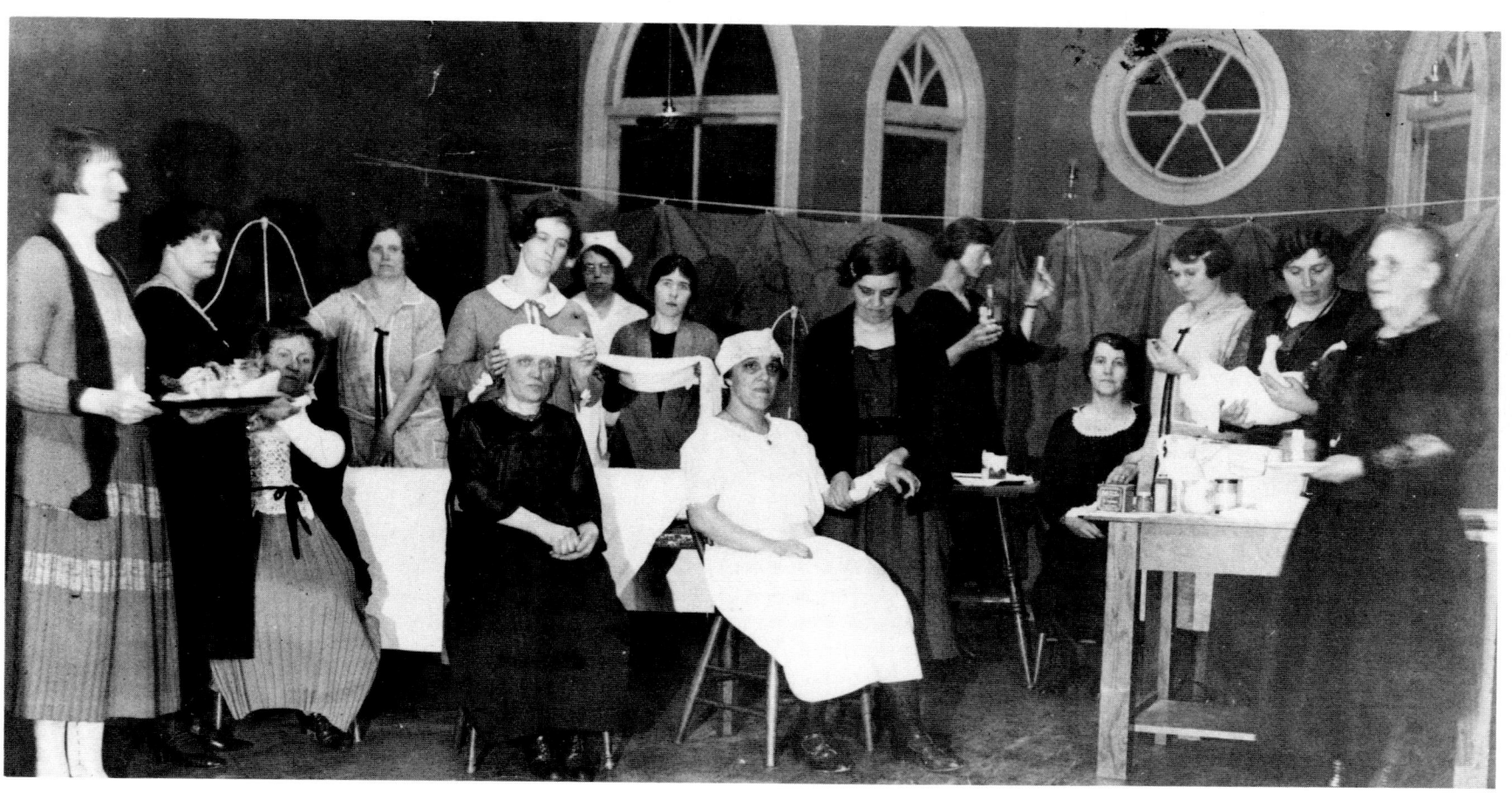

"If the Klondike gold rush was the inferno that forged Skagway, then the second World War was the inferno that reshaped it all over again," says councilman Steve Hites, who is helping prepare the city's 1992 activities commemorating the war years. "World War II made Skagway more of what it is today than people who visit will ever realize."

The war brought massive military projects to fortify the north, including construction of the Alaska-Canada Highway and the Canada Oil (Canol) Pipeline. The highway would provide overland access to strategic northern air bases; the pipeline project included a crude oil refinery to be built at Whitehorse and a fuel pipeline from coast to interior.

FACING PAGE: *The Fraternal Order of Eagles was one of the first organizations in Skagway. For this August 1909 photo, members of the Skagway F. O. E. Aerie No. 25 turned out to pose with the organization's national leader, Grandworthy President Frank E. Hering and his party.* (Courtesy of Mrs. James Doogan)

Skagway was a key port of entry for highway construction crews and supplies headed to Whitehorse, from where construction would go north and south. Skagway also was the terminus for the Canol pipeline.

As soon as the people of Skagway heard about Pearl Harbor, they sensed Skagway with its port and railroad could become a key component of the war effort in Alaska. They formed a Civilian Defense Committee. Fire extinguishers and barrels of sand were put in public buildings and homes. Townspeople took turns guarding the Signal Corps station, which provided Skagway's communication with Outside. Spring 1942 brought construction of the much-talked about Alaska-Canada Highway.

In a matter of months, 12,000 troops came ashore in the town of then-600. The military had been in Skagway before: During the gold rush, four companies totaling about 400 men had been in Skagway and Dyea a few months until the Spanish-American War in 1898 took most of them away. After the war, an infantry unit—one of four black Army units—was sent to Skagway where it remained until 1902. During World War I, soldiers had been sent to guard the railroad. But the military presence in earlier times was nothing to compare with what happened in 1942.

From a tent city at the airport, the Army threw up hundreds of barracks and Quonset huts on every vacant parcel of land in town and took over abandoned gold rush saloons, hotels and other buildings. Fires became regular occurrences as troops lit stoves unused for decades. The grand Elks Lodge burned this way, the flames fueled by a strong north wind. The daily arrival of dozens of steamships, barges and freighters clogged the bay. Skagway's waterfront rumbled around the clock. Barges tied up around the point were brought back and forth with tugs, and the military bulldozed a section of beach where the barges could be pushed ashore and unloaded. In September 1942, Skagway became an Army subport of Seattle. The 348th Longshore Battalion, composed of five companies, brought order to the chaos. Solving the bottlenecks in Skagway provided training early on to longshoring troops who later unloaded the war machine at Allied ports worldwide.

There were few limits on the creativity of Skagway's residents in the years after the gold rush. Costume parties were a regular occurrence, and Edna Feero, daughter of John Feero, took a prize for the most original costume when she came as an umbrella to a 1924 party. (Courtesy of Mrs. James Doogan)

Through Skagway came the 73rd Light Pontoon Company and Company D of the 29th Topographic Battalion, the 18th Engineer Combat Regiment, the 93rd Engineer General Service Regiment, the 340th Engineer General Service Regiment. Of the 340th, one platoon remained in Skagway for the duration, another went to Whitehorse and the remaining regiment ended up at Lake Teslin. The 770th Railroad Operating Battalion made

Skagway its headquarters and took over operation of the 110-mile White Pass and Yukon Route. Civilian construction crews flooded into town, too. Civilian contractors working out of Skagway included the Kansas City Bridge Co. and Bechtel-Price-Callahan, a joint venture of nine companies: W.A. Bechtel Co. and Bechtel Co., both of San Francisco; H.C. Price Co., Bartlesville, Ok.; W.E. Callahan Construction Co., Dallas; J.H. Pomeroy and Co., San Francisco; Gunther and Shirley Co., B.M.P. Co., and Paul Grafe, of Los Angeles; and R.A. Conyes, San Pablo, Calif. The Bechtel venture worked on the Canol project, responsible for design of the refinery, crude pipeline and pumping stations and construction of the project.

When the Canol pipeline from Skagway to Whitehorse began summer 1942, crowded facilities in town became even more so. The Army erected a tent city to house the workers and leased 30 buildings in town, including the Golden North Hotel and the Pullen House.

In the meantime, Skagway women knitted and sewed for the soldiers. They formed a civilian patrol, walking the beach with military-issue binoculars and identification guides to enemy aircraft and ships, according to late resident Betty Selmer. The Women's Club raised money to buy equipment for the new 150-bed Army hospital. Someone donated a building for a USO center. Water and sewer systems were upgraded during this time to solve sanitation problems brought by the ballooning population, and the city shared its only fire truck with the Army. Martin Itjen's streetcar was commandeered as a military shuttle serving the bars and barracks. While the town patriotically supported the troops, it later filed $177,500 in claims against the War Department for costs associated with the occupation.

After the War

The pullout of troops left Skagway quiet and largely depressed. The Army had taken most of the Quonset huts; townspeople took apart many of the wooden barracks

Skagway boasted several newspapers in its early years. Here William Keller, wearing a derby, inspects operations at the Daily Alaskan *about 1910. Edna Black Feero, wife of Frank Feero, worked as bookkeeper and cashier at the paper for four years.* (Courtesy of Mrs. James Doogan)

Native children from many Alaska communities attended the St. Pius X Mission boarding school at 15th and State streets. Opened in 1933 by Rev. G. Edgar Gallant, the school was staffed by sisters from the Order of St. Ann's in Victoria, B.C. By the 1940s, the school's enrollment had doubled to 80 and high school classes were added. The school closed in 1959, but services continued to be held in the mission chapel until the 1970s. After it was abandoned, the building fell into disrepair and was destroyed in a 1985 fire. (Courtesy of Mrs. James Doogan)

and used the planks to enlarge or reface their houses. By the time the military turned the railroad back to civilian management in May 1946, the equipment was worn out. Business was at an ebb, both for the railroad and the town. The three groceries in town that had done a booming business during the war now found enough customers for only one. The abandoned Army hospital was turned into a tuberculosis sanatorium to serve southeastern Alaska. And for a time, a limited amount of lumbering was done in the Taiya River valley. Ed Hosford operated the Skagway Lumber Co. sawmill a few miles up the Chilkoot trail in the late 1950s. Hosford and Andrew Mahle also logged state timber sales in the valley for a few years.

One of the few going concerns after the

war was the St. Pius X Mission, a Catholic boarding school for needy children. The school had opened fall 1933 and operated until 1959. The Rev. G. Edgar Gallant, the first priest ordained in Alaska, raised money to build the school. He worked on the railroad as a young man, joined a Jesuit order in Oregon, and returned as priest for Skagway and Haines. Gallant provided opportunities for the Native children attending the school at a time when discrimination was commonplace in the territory. For instance, he started a scout troop for the mission children in the 1930s when they were not allowed to join the scout troop in town, according to an article in the 1985 *Skaguay Alaskan*. A fire in winter 1945 displaced the children to the Liarsville sanatorium, then to abandoned Army barracks on Broadway until the dorms were rebuilt. Byron Mallott, who later became one of the state's foremost Native leaders, attended the school. Gallant left Skagway for Anchorage in the 1950s, after he became monsignor, and enrollment dropped as new public schools opened in southeastern Alaska and a new boarding school opened in the Interior. Only 20 children attended the mission school during its final year.

During the late 1940s, Skagway began to buzz with talk of an industrial megaproject in the nearby Taiya River valley. Following the war, the U.S. Bureau of Reclamation began looking to Alaska with its many rivers as sources of water for hydroelectric generation, irrigation and other uses. One of the many projects the bureau suggested was the diversion of water from the Lewes River (Upper Yukon) drainage basin in Canada to the Taiya River, north of Skagway. The plans called for a series of dams on the Lewes River above Whitehorse to make a giant reservoir that would be tapped at Lake Lindeman in British Columbia, the water brought to the Taiya River through 15 miles of tunnel under the Coast Range. The project's potential was mind-boggling; the total drop would have been more than 13 times the height of Niagara Falls and at least four

As one of the most important communities in Southeast, Skagway was proud of the basketball teams fielded by its high school. On the women's basketball team in 1930 (shown above) were: front, left to right: Geraldine Feero, Myrna Feero, Alice Storey; back, left to right: Pauline Selmer, Winnie Sipprell, Margery Goding, Haleen Johnston, and coach Virginia Selmer. Pauline and Virginia were sisters. Their brother, Oscar, later married Alice Storey. The 1929 men's basketball team, shown on the facing page, included front, left to right: Clair Richter, Ward McAllister, Selby Phelps, Jack Lee; back, left to right: Bud Blanchard, Wilfred Goding, Walt Sipprell and Lewis Dahl, who later became a doctor at Johns Hopkins. (Courtesy of Mrs. James Doogan)

times the crest of Grand Coulee Dam.

The federal and territorial governments promoted it seriously. Nearly 46,600 acres of land in the Taiya River basin were withdrawn under a public land order, and the Aluminum Company of America leased land at Dyea and Skagway with plans to build a hydroelectric power plant and an aluminum smelter producing 400 million pounds of metal a year. The project would have employed 4,000 workers and transformed Skagway into a booming industrial community of 20,000 to 40,000 people, according to published reports at the time.

The Canadian government, however, was not too keen on draining the headwaters of its Yukon River for America's benefit, and in 1953 nixed ALCOA's application for a project permit. The project continued to elicit discussion on the Alaska side through the mid-1960s.

Tourism Comes of Age

For many years, it was impossible to consider activity in Skagway without considering the White Pass and Yukon Route. But regular state ferry service started in 1963 and ushered in a new era of tourism, supplementing railroad and longshoring activities. The service connected Skagway to other southeastern Alaska cities, Seattle, and Prince Rupert, B.C., and allowed tourists to remain in Skagway longer. At this time, the railroad carried nearly 45,000 tourists a year from Skagway to Lake Bennett.

Another boost to tourism came in 1977 with the opening of the Klondike Gold Rush National Historical Park. It brought more local jobs and helped stabilize the historic downtown as the National Park Service began restoring gold-rush-era buildings. Then in 1979, Skagway became accessible to visitors by car and motorcoach with completion to Whitehorse of the 99-mile Klondike Highway 2. By 1980,

Vic Sparks displays his version of Sparky, modeled after a comic strip horse and outfitted like a gold rush pack-train animal, in about 1925. Sparky stood for many years in front of the A. B. Hall, and today can be seen at Tent City. (Courtesy of Mrs. James Doogan)

tourism provided about 30 percent of the community's local revenues.

The highway had been under construction on the American side since the late 1950s. Carl Mulvihill, who was born in Skagway, remembers a cat road when he was in high school in the late 1950s. Each election year, he said, the state chipped away at building the road. By 1961, about four-and-a-half miles were completed out of Skagway. Another mile was added the next year and another eight-tenths of a mile in 1963. The Canadian government got behind the road in the late 1970s and it was completed to Carcross. It opened for a month in 1978, then closed for winter. In 1986, it was opened year-round. Mulvihill also said in the 1920s the local residents began building a road on the east side of the Skagway River, heading toward Warm Pass. They completed about five miles. In the 1940s, the White Pass and Yukon Route bought part of the property. The road can still be found today, although it is overgrown.

Talk of a proposed natural gas pipeline in the early 1980s, to run from Alaska's North Slope through Canada, stirred speculation that Skagway would be the transshipment point for pipeline construction materials, by rail or truck. Likewise, proposals to extend the railroad line 150 miles to Faro, to be closer to large mineral deposits, spurred other hopes for Skagway's economy.

But the shutdown in 1982 of the White Pass rail line, triggered by closure the Cyprus Anvil lead-zinc mine in the Yukon — the railroad's biggest freight customer — brought near-panic to town. The city scrambled for new industries. It tested a wind generator. It tried to attract the state's new maximum security prison, which went to Seward. A seafood processing plant was discussed. But the upper Taiya Inlet has never supported any commercial fisheries, only a modest subsistence and sport fishery. The town boasted its pure water to brewery developers, only to find its water was not so pure. An effort to legalize gambling was considered and rejected. The only thing that seemed to be working for Skagway was tourism.

A shot in its industrial arm came in 1985 when Toronto-based Curragh Resources Corp. bought and reopened the Cyprus Anvil mine. This prompted opening the Klondike Highway 2 for year-round use, and Curragh began shipping its ore concentrate through Skagway, trucked to town by Lynden Inc. The move to open the highway year-round to trucks was loudly opposed by many in Skagway for a variety of reasons,

Marian Katseek Kelm

By Su Rappleye

Marian Katseek Kelm is an Alaskan Native, one of the few who lives in Skagway. "I was born on October 15th, 1931. I was raised in Haines until we moved down to Klukwan. I went to school there, and discovered I had a bad ear infection so I lost my hearing. I went as far as eighth grade, and that was it. We stayed out in Klukwan where I helped my mom; she taught us how to do the beading. My dad taught us how to do totem pole painting."

"In 1973, Ernie and me tied the knot. From Haines we went to Fairbanks and then Anchorage because he was with immigration. Then my mom (Margaret Katseek) wanted to come to Skagway. Her mother (Ann Gordon) was buried here in the old cemetery, as were her sister and a niece. We asked her where she wanted to go because the Haines station was open. My mom said, 'We'll gamble on Skagway.' So we brought her over here, and she stayed with us for 12 years. She was 94 when she passed away.

"Skagway seems like a real nice place to live. It's changed quite a bit from my childhood days. I used to remember where the railroad tracks came up the middle of Broadway. My mom and dad used to bring us over to see cousins."

"I used to be so scared when we got on Mr. Rapuzzi's streetcar — there was a dummy standing in the back of it. Every time my mom tried to get us on the streetcar so we could come uptown, I'd just cry; I was afraid of it."

"Then my dad used to tell us: 'You can't come in your aunt's place cause it's adults-talking day only, no children allowed.' And my dad would give us quarters and tell us to go down to the taffy store, and buy a bag of taffy to take home."

Not all of Marian's memories are so pleasant. It was not popular to be Indian when she was growing up, and she was often the victim of discrimination. "I couldn't go to the same classroom with the white kids. If we spoke our language in the classroom, we got our mouth wiped out with soap and sent home. We could not go to school dances with the white students; couldn't go to the theater with the whites."

The union of Marian and her husband, Ernie, has bridged two cultures. Ernie had already been adopted by the Tlingits, and was studying their culture and language when his first wife passed away. Later he proposed, and Marian accepted. She speaks highly of his three children and four grandchildren, who are just as much hers now as his. Together they have taught their family and much of the Skagway community about Tlingit customs.

Marian's Native name is Cosghat, which translates to Blueberry. Ernie explains that the Tlingits do not have royalty, but if they did, Marian would be a princess of the Kiksadi Clan. Out of 10 children, Marian has two brothers and one sister still living. She says she is not the eldest, but that she remembers the most of what they were taught as youngsters. …

"Dad used to tell us stories. He used to have us sit at the table at breakfast time and we got a big lecture. Just like having class. My brother always says he doesn't know anything about it. I say you're supposed to remember. Momma used to tell us girls, and we remember what she said. It's supposed to be the same for the boys. When dad takes you out fishing and hunting and tells you these stories, you're supposed to remember."

Marian worked for years as a chef. "I worked in the road place at 33 mile, doing short order meals for a buck and a half. Finally one day I said to myself: For 12 years I've been getting the same pay so it's time to find another job. I worked at the Halsingland Hotel in Haines. I worked in the schools doing lunches for the students in Haines and Klukwan."

She teases Ernie these days that maybe she'll open a pizza parlor, but she also speaks of someday writing a book.

"I'd write it on how we grew up, what kind of houses we lived in, what kind of clothes we wore, what kind of food we ate. Now we're eating white man's food, and we're all dying off from cancer. We never even knew anything about cancer cause we lived off the land. We have our moose meat, and deer meat, and sheep meat, goat meat, and fish — all kinds of fish, smoked salmon, salted salmon — all the seafood you could get. There was no such thing as coming down with a cold or anything like that. That's how come our people lived are so healthy, because they eat off the land."

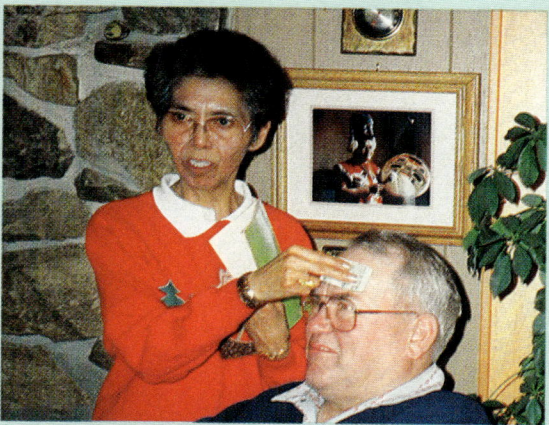

Tlingit Marian Katseek Kelm, one of the few Alaskan Natives to reside in Skagway, recalls both the good times and bad in her adopted hometown. Discrimination in years past limited some of her activities, but she says times have changed. Marian and her husband, Ernie, teach others in Skagway about the Tlingit culture. (Courtesy of Marian Kelm)

In 1991, nearly half the town's 315,000 visitors arrived by cruise ships. Here the Sun Viking *and* Regent Star *moor at the Broadway Dock.* (Harry M. Walker)

including increased traffic and noise.

By the time White Pass reopened its railroad to passengers in 1988, Skagway was well-established as one of Alaska's most popular tourist destinations. Developing Skagway as a visitor destination and seeing the railroad return were among the town's hardest-won successes.

Not surprisingly then, local people were not pleased when lead contamination in town became widely publicized in Alaska in the late 1980s. Locally, the possibility of lead dust contamination had been recognized for decades. Townspeople had smelled ore and seen dust billowing from the terminal for years, and then-mayor Bill Feero recalled hooking bags of lead as a longshoreman. But involvement of the federal Environmental Protection Agency and the state Department of Environmental Conservation brought soil sampling to town — at the terminal, along the highway, railroad tracks and around some homes. Curragh Resources and White Pass launched a cleanup program that included giant vacuum trucks to remove contaminated soil. In a wry moment, Chamber of Commerce president Suzanne Mullen suggested putting lead dust in little vials, labeled with the slogan, "I got the lead out in Skagway." Two rounds of blood tests were given to about 250 of the town's residents, including all the children; in late 1989, the state said no health problem existed, although it outlined a list of precautions such as frequent mopping and dusting, not wearing street shoes inside houses and rinsing homegrown vegetables before eating. The citizen's group, "Get the Lead Out," disbanded in early 1990.

Although the community was given a clean bill of health, the problem was one of the most expensive and laborious cleanups of industrial pollution in the state. The companies involved spent about $6 million. In addition, the Alaska Industrial Development and Export Authority spent $25 million to purchase, renovate and expand the ore terminal. As part of this, the terminal was enclosed and equipped with self-contained air filters. Curragh signed a long-term lease to repay the state's investment, and in late 1991 increased shipments through the port with ore from its new Sa Dena Hes - Mount Hundere lead-zinc mine north of Watson Lake.

Today the people of Skagway look to continued success as a tourist destination — in 1991, the White Pass carried a record 100,000-plus passengers. Yet, the need for year-round employment remains strong. Currently, full-time jobs year-round exist at the school, the National Park Service, the U.S. Customs and Immigration offices, the state highway department and several companies directly associated with freighting and transshipments. White Pass Transportation operates all docks except the city's, runs a fleet of trucks to haul goods and fuel into Canada, operates the twice-monthly freighter *Frank Brown*, and operates the fuel pipeline and pumping station. Fairways Fast Freight, a local subsidiary of Lynden, Inc., handles the Alaska Marine Lines barge that brings supplies to town each week, and Bowhead Equipment Co. runs the ore terminal.

With the goal of community growth and year-round jobs in mind, the Alaska Power and Telephone Co. plans a $10 million hydroelectric plant at Goat Lake, near Pitchfork Falls about 3,000 feet above town. The plant would supplement current sources — a 1909 hydrosystem that draws from Lower Dewey Lake and freezes in winter, and diesel-powered generators. "It's the idea that Skagway is going to grow,

LEFT: *The Golden North, Alaska's oldest operating hotel, stands at the corner of Third Avenue and Broadway Street. It was built in 1898 by the Klondike Trading Company as a two-story structure. George Dedman and Edward Foreman bought the building in 1908 and moved it to its present location. They added a third floor, raised the corner dome another story and outfitted the business as a hotel, at the time Alaska's largest.* (Harry M. Walker)

BELOW: *The Arctic Brotherhood Hall, built in 1899, is a unique example of rustic Victorian architecture. The Brotherhood fraternal organization originated Feb. 26, 1899, with 11 men traveling to Skagway on the City of Seattle. Membership grew to about 300 and 30 other camps sprang up along the route to the Klondike. Charles O. Walker created the building's driftwood mosaic facade.* (Harry M. Walker)

and growth depends on power at a reliable rate," says Alan See, Alaska Power and Telephone vice president of operations.

Skagway also is promoting itself to people who enjoy winter. The Buckwheat Ski Classic, with several long-distance Nordic events, is an international draw each year in late March, usually the weekend after the town's Windfest celebration. In the making are visitor packages to include lodging, snow machining and skiing. The town's abundance of hotel rooms may be

Paul Jones

By Su Rappleye

Paul Jones showed up on the old Chilkat ferry for a quick look around at Skagway in 1958, and three years later he had moved here for good. PJ, as he is known, says he made the move because there were fewer people, and he quickly moved again from Skagway to Dyea for the same reason; he's not a town person. "When I first moved out to live in Dyea, Emil Hanousek and I were the only ones there. And then after he had a stroke and they sent him off to Juneau, I was the only one there for four or five years."

PJ has a slow and quiet way about him. At 64, he lives alone in Dyea with no phone, and no generator for electricity. He uses a Coleman lamp or kerosene for light; a barrel woodstove for heat and cooking; and a nearby spring for refrigeration. He has two large garden plots, where he grows all the vegetables he needs including "cabbages, turnips, potatoes, lots of potatoes, carrots, onions, a little bit of everything but good tomatoes. The garden takes up all my summer; in the winter I cut a little wood and sit by the fire and read. I read almost anything that's readable, as long as it's not science fiction."

PJ's also the mayor. "I inherited the title of Mayor of Dyea from Emil. There's no duties involved; it's just an honorary deal. I don't know how long Emil was mayor, but he'd been in Dyea for several years, and I've been mayor for 15 years or so. Probably just five people live in Dyea year-round now, and they don't come to me unless they really have bad problems, like somebody gets stuck in a mud hole or something, then they might come get me."

When he first moved to Dyea, PJ lived in a two-story house out on the flats, but that house burned down, and since then he has lived on land belonging to Malcolm Moe. "The house where I'm living now was an old Army barracks building from Skagway. They floated it around on a barge. The road only went as far as Long Bay and then you walked over the hill on the trail. It used to be an old poker house. All the older guys, Malcolm Moe and Morgan Reed, this is where they all used to go to play poker. When I put new insulation in the building, I found a pint of whiskey. Hard to tell how long that was there."

Quick with stories about other people but slow to talk about himself, PJ just says he did a little bit of everything when he first arrived, and then adds how it was when he bartended for the Pack Train Inn. "There were about five local guys that were here in town that cleared the bar out every time they come in. Everybody would leave just to get away from them. So we bartenders would always try to pull one on one another, and we'd always keep $10 back to hand these guys to go to the other bar to have drinks."

PJ says he only worked for a few years after he came to Alaska, moving from one job to another for variety, and then one day announced he was retired. "I just made up my mind. I'd worked ever since I was a little kid, and I had to work hard. When I was going to high school I had to take care of my folks and drive 40 miles one way back and forth to high school. I'd get up at 4 o'clock and I wouldn't get home til 10. Then I'd do the chores, milk the cows, and this that and the other thing. I finally just made up my mind that I've had it, that's it. You can make enough money just on the side to get by on."

PJ admits he was born on Valentine's Day, 1927, and raised on a cattle ranch in the Green Horn Mountains of the high Sierras of southern California, where his grandparents had been some of the first

Dyea, now the year-round home of only a handful of residents, is the starting point for hikers headed up the Chilkoot trail. (Ernest Manewal)

to settle. PJ flew jet fighters out of Kodo, Japan from 1949 to 1951. He says his plane was hit once over the Korean coast, but "you can fly a long ways at 600 mph." His plane went into the ocean right alongside an aircraft carrier. "Plane never even had time to sink; helicopter was right there."

PJ has two daughters and three grandchildren in Washington state, but says he has not regretted his move to Alaska. "I've been very happy here. This is a good crowd that lives in this country. It's sort of changed some here in the last five to 10 years, but that's because a lot of people that come here just come in for summer work and then they're gone. But then I don't come to town that much in the summertime; I make sure it's just about a non-boat day. [A day in which no cruise ships come into Skagway.] I get the boat schedule and I put it on the wall."

"It's an enjoyable life, and I plan to just stay here until I get so decrepit I can't hardly move and then I'm going to Washington and let the kids take care of me."

The Klondike Highway 2 between Skagway and Whitehorse offers spectacular scenery. This view shows a stretch of road just north of the U.S. Customs station near Skagway. In 1991, the customs office counted 111,000 vehicles on the road, most of them during summer. During winter, the highway becomes the state's most expensive to maintain, largely because of blowing snow at the summit. It is kept open to accommodate ore trucks traveling between Canadian mines and the Skagway port. "One thing about the truck traffic," said U.S. Customs port director Boyd Worley, "If you break down or get stuck in a snow bank, there will be someone along. They all have telephones in their trucks and are good about helping." Dense fog during winter also can make driving tedious. An older woman motorist once asked Worley with no small degree of irritation: "Why did you all build that road in the fog anyway?" (Harry M. Walker)

its ticket to off-season conventions, such as the 1992 Alaska Visitor's Association meeting scheduled in Skagway.

In summer 1992, the number of visitors is expected to increase with the anniversary of the Alaska Highway construction. A multimedia presentation in Arctic Brotherhood Hall, a walking tour of historical buildings from that era, and a restored Quonset hut added to the wartime exhibit outside the city museum are among the anniversary doings that add to Skagway's gold rush lure.

"People here are proud of their heritage and the contributions Skagway has made in Alaska," says tourism director Fuqua. "Just walking around town gives you the sense that those days must have been really wild."

Klondike Gold Rush National Historical Park

The Klondike Gold Rush National Historical Park anchors Skagway's historic district and enhances the town's appeal to visitors. Its opening summer 1977 brought a new dimension to the town's tourism, adding jobs and a federal management plan to bear on development of Skagway's downtown. With Skagway as its centerpiece, the park also encompasses the Chilkoot and the White Pass trails and Pioneer Square in Seattle, where many stampeders boarded boats for Alaska.

The park culminated a 40-year vision. The idea of a national park or monument commemorating Skagway's role in the Klondike gold rush started being tossed around by the town's residents in the early 1930s. In fall 1933, Alaska territorial Gov. John Weir Troy and Skagway lawyer-banker Edward A. Rasmuson discussed the economic value such a park could bring to southeastern Alaska. The Skagway Chamber of Commerce assigned Rasmuson, W.C. Blanchard and Rev. G. Edgar Gallant to the project. Working with territorial Congressional delegate Anthony J. Dimond, the men took their proposal to Arno B. Cammerer, director of the National Park Service (NPS), in 1934.

Cammerer was not enthusiastic. He thought the project might be too similar in nature to Glacier Bay National Monument. In the meantime, the idea was getting pushed from another direction. Influential geographer Wallace Atwood, who was president of Clark University in Worcester, Mass. and a member of the Advisory Board on National Parks, Historic Sites, Buildings and Monuments, saw the area's potential as a national or international park. He suggested the idea to Cammerer. Again Cammerer nixed it.

Atwood pushed ahead anyway. He proposed creation of a Chilkoot Trail national or international park to U.S. Sec. of Interior Harold Ickes. The idea enchanted Ickes, and he directed Cammerer to look into it. The resulting report came back mostly negative. Cammerer's project reviewers ignored the historical and cultural significance of the Skagway region, tagged the inholdings of the town and railroad as undesirable, and said other areas in Southeast had more spectacular scenery. But the advisory board basically ignored the report, and appointed a committee that included Atwood to study the project further.

In the 1950s during Mayor Cy Coyne's tenure, Skagway residents began to seek attention for its history. The city established a historical commission and asked the National Park Service to again

The restored White Pass and Yukon Route railroad depot houses the Klondike Gold Rush National Historical Park visitor center. Depot construction began May 1898 and by December, a ticket office, waiting room and baggage room had opened on the first floor. On interior walls, visitors can see reproductions of original wallpaper — described by one gold-rush-era reporter as a "symphony of green and gold." (Ernest Manewal)

look at the area. In July 1961, Charles Snell of the National Survey of Historic Sites and Buildings visited Skagway. Its gold rush aura entranced him. Snell suggested that the area be added to the national park system. He also recommended the town be nominated as a National Historic Landmark and Chilkoot Pass be given Landmark Status.

At its 1962 annual meeting, the advisory board recognized the historical significance of Skagway and White Pass, and U.S. Sec. of Interior Stewart L. Udall declared them

Here at The Scales, a half-mile below Chilkoot Pass, gold rush stampeders repacked their loads for the final climb. Its name derived from the packers, who reweighed their freight here and usually upped their rates for the summit push. It was known as "one of the most wretched spots on the trail." (Harry M. Walker)

BELOW: *Gold rush stampeders carried these collapsible canoes to the summit of the Chilkoot Pass, but then abandoned them. Perhaps the Canadian North West Mounted Police confiscated the canoes because they were too flimsy to withstand the treacherous rapids of the Yukon waterways.* (Ernest Manewal)

RIGHT: *Relics from the gold rush abound along the Chilkoot trail. An old tramway boiler at Canyon City attracts the attention of Harry M. Walker, photographer and former Skagway resident.* (Harry M. Walker)

eligible to be National Historic Landmarks. The board also recommended that Skagway be added to the national park system. During the year, the Alaska Department of Natural Resources put prison inmates to work clearing and restoring the Chilkoot trail to the border. With the National Historic Landmark designation, local property owners could obtain federal and state historic preservation loans and grants.

The NPS conducted field work in the Skagway region, summers 1967 through 1969. This included a joint visit by American and Canadian park officials. In 1968, the Yukon Territory corrections department, in cooperation with British Columbia, began restoring the Canadian side of the Chilkoot and by summer 1969, the entire Chilkoot was open as a recreational trail. In December 1969, U.S. Sec. of Interior Walter Hickel announced that the NPS was interested in developing a National Historical Park in Skagway and the surrounding region. In 1976, Congress passed legislation creating the Klondike Gold Rush National Historical Park.

Today, the park includes four units: Skagway, Seattle, the Chilkoot Trail and the White Pass Trail. In addition, the Canadian Parks Service administers the Chilkoot trail from the international border

Hikers reaching the summit of Chilkoot Pass find this plaque commemorating the thousands of stampeders who made their way over the pass. (David Rhode)

to Lake Bennett, B.C. Staff from the appropriate park services are located year-round in Skagway and Whitehorse and during summer at Dyea, Sheep Camp, Chilkoot summit and Lindeman City. Also in summer, rangers hike the Chilkoot trail to provide information and assistance.

The Park Units

The Skagway unit covers an eight-block historic district downtown. The park service visitor center is located in the original White Pass depot on Broadway Street. More than 50 downtown buildings — variously owned by private individuals, the city and the park service — contribute to Skagway's listing on the National Register of Historic Places. A number of them are open to the public. Eleven of the park service's 16 historic buildings are restored, and work is currently underway on the Lynch and Kennedy Dry Goods store. The park service's next project is to restore the Peniel Mission in 1993. An architectural historian on staff oversees the work, and archaeologists excavate around the foundations prior to restoration.

The White Pass Trail unit extends from the site of White Pass City to the summit of White Pass. But this unit is the park's least developed. About the only way to see this part of the park is by train. The White Pass and Yukon Route tracks pass through the middle of its 3,320 acres. Remnants of the gold rush, such as Brackett's wagon road and Dead Horse Gulch, can be seen out the train's windows.

Local people have expressed interest in the park service developing a walk-in campground at historic White Pass City, said park superintendent Clay Alderson. This possibility will be explored as part of the park's new management plan, which was in initial stages in early 1992. The park's emphasis has been on developing the downtown historic district and cultural history, Alderson said. The new plan will look at expanding visitor access to remote areas in the park, and how that might affect the land. To that end, the park service will be doing an inventory of the natural resources in its holdings and looking for endangered or threatened species.

The Chilkoot Trail unit follows the Alaska portion of the 33-mile trail from old Dyea to Lake Bennett. This mile-wide, 17-mile-long corridor covers 9,674 acres. This section of the park includes the Dyea townsite and the Slide Cemetery where many of the Palm Sunday avalanche victims are buried. This historic backcountry trail follows the original Chilkoot route where possible. Just as in gold rush days, the Chilkoot's terrain is rough and its weather often extreme. A trip requires careful planning, and should only be attempted by well-equipped hikers in good physical condition. Planning a safe trip over the trail is beyond the scope of this book, but advice is available through the park service and numerous backcountry guidebooks.

The Chilkoot trail drew 2,200 hikers in 1991. More than 3,000 people hiked the trail each year prior to the railroad's shutdown in 1982. Use of the trail diminished considerably during the railroad's six-year hiatus. However, the number of hikers has rebounded since the railroad reopened and returned service to Lake Bennett, where most hikers end their trip and catch the train back.

Gold rush relics litter today's Chilkoot trail. Much of what the stampeders hauled up the trail got left behind. Abandoned sleds, a large iron stove and rusting parts of an old tramway boiler recall the former

FACING PAGE: *Chilkoot trail hikers rest at Pleasant Camp at mile 10.5, one of the first places with level ground north of Canyon City. (Harry M. Walker)*

ALASKA GEOGRAPHIC® 75

This stream flows along Chilkoot trail near Sheep Camp, at mile 13. No camping is allowed on the trail between Sheep Camp and Happy Camp, at mile 20.5. (Harry M. Walker)

glory of Canyon City. Miscellaneous bones and old shoes poke out of the ground along the way. Frames of folding canoes, tools and sled parts evidence past bustle at The Scales. An old tramway tower still stands, and a tramway cable and telegraph wires lie along the ascent to the summit. Interpretative signs erected by the park service help mark the route. No antiques along the trail should be disturbed or removed because of their historical importance.

The Seattle unit of the Klondike Gold Rush National Historical Park is located in Pioneer Square, the heart of gold rush Seattle. The NPS visitor center here is housed in the Union Trust Annex at 117 S. Main Street, about two blocks north of the Kingdome and 1.5 blocks east of the waterfront. The Klondike gold rush helped make Seattle the center of trade in the northwest — by spring 1898 Seattle merchants, who during the previous few years had barely eked out a living, had sold some $25 million in goods. Therefore a park unit was established here to help preserve that legacy. Pioneer Square, with dozens of shops in restored buildings, is where the prospectors bought their supplies, boarded ships berthed nearby and headed north to Dyea and Skagway.

Bibliography

Adney, Edwin Tappan. *The Klondike Stampede of 1897-1898.* Fairfield, Wa.: Ye Galleon Press, 1968.

Bankson, Russell A. *The Klondike Nugget.* Caldwell, Idaho: Caxton Printers, 1935.

Bearss, Edwin C. *Klondike Gold Rush National Historical Park Historic Resource Study.* Washington D.C.: U.S. Dept. of the Interior, National Park Service, 1970.

Becker, Ethel. "A Klondike Woman's Diary," *Alaska* magazine. Anchorage: Alaska Northwest Publishing Co., June 1970.

___. *Klondike '98: E.A. Hegg's Gold Rush Album.* Portland: Binfords & Mort, 1972.

Benedict, G.A. "Skagway Supports War Effort," *Alaska Life.* Juneau: Alaska Life Publishing Co., March 1943.

Berton, Pierre. *The Klondike Fever.* New York: Alfred A. Knopf, 1974.

___. *The Klondike Quest.* Boston/Toronto: Little, Brown and Co. with The Atlantic Monthly Press, 1983.

Brady, Jeff, ed. *Skaguay Alaskan,* summer supplement to *The Skagway News,* various issues, 1980-1990.

___. *The Skagway News,* various issues, 1983-1991.

Bronson, William and Reinhardt, Richard. *The Last Grand Adventure.* New York: McGraw-Hill Book Co., 1977.

Clifford, Howard. *The Skagway Story.* Anchorage: Alaska Northwest Publishing Co., 1975.

Cohen, Stan. *Gold Rush Gateway.* Missoula, Mont.: Pictorial Histories Publishing Co., 1986.

___. *The White Pass and Yukon Route.* Missoula, Mont.: Pictorial Histories Publishing Co., 1980.

DeArmond, R.N., ed. *Klondike Newsman "Stroller" White.* Skagway: Lynn Canal Publishing, 1989.

Eppenbach, Sarah. *Alaska Southeast, Touring the Inside Passage.* Chester, Conn.: The Globe Pequot Press, 1991.

Honius, Ruth Selby. "Historic Skagway," *Alaska Life.* Juneau: Alaska Life Publishing Co., August 1946.

Hunt, William R. *Golden Places, the History of Alaska-Yukon Mining.* Anchorage: National Park Service, Alaska Region, 1990.

Itjen, Martin. *The Story of the Tour on the Skagway, Alaska, Street Car.* 1962.

Kalen, Barbara. "Castle Kern," *Alaska Sportsman.* Anchorage: Alaska Northwest Publishing Co., May 1962.

Martin, Cy. *Gold Rush Narrow Gauge.* Los Angeles: Trans-Anglo Books, 1969.

Mayer, Melanie J. *Klondike Women, True Tales of the 1897-1898 Gold Rush.* Athens, Ohio: Swallow Press/Ohio University Press, 1989.

McCready, Martha. *Gateway to Gold.* Whitehorse, Yukon: Studio North Ltd., 1990.

Minter, Roy. *The White Pass, Gateway to the Klondike.* Fairbanks: University of Alaska Press, 1987.

Moore, Bernard J. *Skagway In Days Primeval.* New York: Vantage Press, 1968.

Norris, Frank. "Martin Itjen, Alaska Tourism Pioneer." Paper presented at Alaska Historical Society annual meeting, Wrangell, Alaska. October 1985.

Neuberger, Richard L. "Alaska Comes of Age," *Argus,* Vol. 59, No. 52. Seattle: Argus Publishing Co., Dec. 13, 1952.

Ogilvie, William. *Early Days on the Yukon.* London: John Lane Publishers, 1913.

___. *The Klondike Official Guide.* Toronto: The Hunter, Rose Co., Ltd., 1898.

Piggott, Margaret. *Discover Southeast Alaska with Pack & Paddle.* Seattle: The Mountaineers, 1990.

Rickard, T.A. *Through the Yukon and Alaska.* San Francisco: Mining and Scientific Press, 1909.

Satterfield, Archie. *Chilkoot Pass.* Anchorage: Alaska Northwest Publishing Co., 1983.

Sherpy, M.L., ed. *The Skaguay News,* various issues, 1897 and 1898.

Skagway Comprehensive Plan, Skagway Planning Commission and Alaska State Housing Authority, March 1964.

Spray, Lafe Eakin. "Skagway, Gem of Alaska," *Alaska-Yukon Magazine,* November 1911.

Smith, Becky. "Prohibition in Alaska," *The Alaska Journal,* Vol. 3, No 3. Anchorage: Alaska Northwest Publishing Co., 1973.

Spude, Robert L.S. *Skagway, District of Alaska 1884-1912.* Fairbanks: University of Alaska and Alaska Regional Office of the National Park Service, 1983.

Tower, Elizabeth A. *Big Mike Heney, Irish Prince of the Iron Rails.* Anchorage: 1988.

Wickersham, James. *Old Yukon, Tales, Trails and Trials.* Washington, D.C.: Washington Law Book Co., 1938.

Woodman, Lt. Col. Lyman. Unpublished manuscript *Duty Station Northwest, the U.S. Army in Alaska and Canada, 1867-1987.*

Index

A.B. Mountain 51
Abbott Detroit Bulldog 55
Adney, Edwin Tappan 17, 18, 23, 26
Alaska Commercial Co. 12
Alaska Industrial Development and Export Authority 66
Alaska Marine Lines 67
Alaska Power and Telephone Co. 67
Alaska-Canada (Alcan) Highway 6, 33, 41, 44, 58, 59
Alaska-Yukon Pacific Exposition 39
Alderson, Clay 74
Allen, Eugene 15
Aluminum Company of America 63
American Teamsters' Union 35
Arctic Brotherhood (A.B.) Hall 51, 64, 67, 69
Ask, Harry 34
Atlin gold rush 31
Atwood, Wallace 70

Beardslee, Lester A 11
Bearss, Edwin 31
Bechtel-Price-Callahan 60
Ben-My-Chree 33
Bigger Hammer Construction Co. 53
Bigger Hammer Marching Band 53
Billinghurst, E.E. 15
Black, Ethel 25, 27
Black, George 26, 39, 50
Black, Grandma 27
Black, Lillian 39
Black, Mr. 21
Blanchard, Bud 62
Blanchard, George 41
Blanchard, W.C. 70
Blanchard, Will and Ann 40, 41
Bookwalter, Vernon 32, 33
Booth, Evangeline 55
Bowhead Equipment Co. 67
Brackett's wagon road 15, 27, 28, 30-32, 74
Brackett, George 28, 30
Brady, Jeff 2
Broadway Street 2, 8, 30, 34, 41, 42, 51, 52, 65

Bronson, William 10, 18
Brooks, Joe 23
Brown, Beriah 8
Brown, George D. 55
Buckwheat 53
Buckwheat Ski Classic 46, 67

Cammerer, Arno B. 70
Canada Oil (Canol) pipeline 6, 33, 41, 58-60
Canadian Bank of Commerce robbery 56
Canyon City 18, 20, 28, 73, 76
Car race 55
Caribou Crossing (Carcross) 32
Carmack, George Washington 15, 26
Case, W.H. 49
Century Magazine 21
Chilkat Glacier 51
Chilkat Indians 12
Chilkat River 11
Chilkoot Indians 10, 12
Chilkoot Pass 8, 12, 16
Chilkoot Pass 4, 6, 11, 13, 18, 25, 26, 72-74
Chilkoot trail 51, 68, 70, 73, 74, 76
Circle City 15
City of Seattle 31, 67
Clark, Henry C. 39
Clinton Creek Mine (asbestos) 36
Close Brothers Co. 30
Coast Mountains 2, 4, 10, 18, 62
Company D, 29th Topographic Battalion 59
Construction, railroad 30, 31
Cowper, Gov. Steve 41
Coyne, Cy 70
Cruise ships 37
Curragh Resources Corp. 64, 66, 67
Cyprus Anvil Mine 35, 36, 64

Dahl, Lewis 62
Daily Alaskan 24, 39, 40, 60
Davenport, Babe 17
Dawson City 10, 12, 15, 16, 20, 33, 40

"Days of '98" Show 51
De Gruyter, Mrs. Jeannette 40
Dead Horse Gulch 74
Dead Horse Trail 21
Dedman's Photo Shop 46, 50
Dedman, Clara 40
Dedman, George 40, 67
Dené Athabaskan Indians 10
Dennis, Silas 2
Dickson, George 12
Dimond, Anthony J. 70
Diyéi 11
Dorn, Mrs. 57
Dunn, Maurice 31
Durham, Walter F. "Bull" 34
Dyea 4, 11-13, 16, 21, 25-28, 32, 38, 44, 56, 59, 63, 68, 74
Dyea Bay 44
Dyea Canyon 20
Dyea Press 26
Dyea River 11, 39

18th Engineer Combat Regiment 59
Excelsior 8, 15

Fairbanks News Miner 47
Fairways Fast Freight 67
Feero pack train 23
Feero, Bill 49, 66
Feero, Edith 24
Feero, Edna Black 25, 27, 57, 59, 60
Feero, Emma Babcock 23, 57
Feero, Frank 23, 50, 60
Feero, Geraldine 62
Feero, John E. 23, 24, 59
Feero, Myrna 62
Ferry service 63
Finnigan's Point 18
Finnigan, Pat 18
First party over White Pass 15
Floods 20
Florence 25
Foley, Pvt. Howard 33
Food requirements 20
Foreman, Edward 67
Fortymile 12, 15

Fourth of July 17, 46, 52
Frank Brown 67
Fraser, B.C. 37
Fraternal Order of Eagles 59
Fuqua, Jerre O'Farrell 2, 47, 69

Gallant, Rev. G. Edgar 61, 62, 70
Garden City of Alaska 6, 38, 40
Gardening 38-41
George W. Elder 15
Georgeson, C.C. 39
Glacier Gorge 36
Glacier Station 2
Glaciers 13, 51
Goding, Margery 62
Goding, Mrs. Blenda 57
Goding, Wilfred 62
Gold Rush Cemetery 51
Golden North Hotel 40, 47, 50, 60, 67
Golden Stairs 18, 28
Gordon, Ann 65
Gordon, Dr. Lamont 45
Grand Tour of Europe 53, 55
Graves, Samuel H. 23, 30
Guthrie, Mrs. Lee 40
Guyer, Mrs. 57

Hall, Ernest 41
Hanousek, Emil 68
Hansen, Ethel Feero 57
Hansen, Nick 49
Hanson, Mrs. Lena 57
Happy Camp 76
Harding, President Warren 51, 56
Harper's Weekly 17
Hartshorn, Florence 18
Hawkins, E.C. 30
Healy, John J. 11, 12, 38
Hegg, E.A. 50
Heney Station 32
Heney, Michael J. 6, 30
Hering, Frank E. 59
Herron, Sam 38
Hickel, Walter 73
Hiking trails 51

Hislop, John 30
Hites, Steve 2, 51, 58
Holmes, H.N. 39
Holt, George 11
Hosford, Ed 61
Hougen, Rolf 37

Ickes, Harold 70
Industrial crash of 1893 8
International Boundary (Canadian) 10
Itjen, Martin 41, 51, 53, 56, 60

Jauxenu, A. 31
Jeff's Parlor 25
Jewell, Charlotte 38, 41
Johnston, Hal Jr. 55
Johnston, Haleen 62
Jones, Paul (PJ) 2, 68
Joy, William H. 39
Juneau Empire 47

Kalen, Barbara Dedman 2, 46, 47
Kalen, Edward J. 46
Kalvick, Edna 41
Kansas City Bridge Co. 60
Katseek, Margaret 65
Keelar, Frank 55
Keller, Dr. L.S. 40
Keller, Myrtle 57
Keller, William 60
Kelm, Ernie 65
Kelm, Marian Katseek 2, 65
Kern's Castle 55
Kern, Peter 55
Kesey, Ken 53
Kirmse, Hazel 39
Kirmse, Herman 39, 41, 55
Kirmse, Jack 39, 55
Klondike Gold Rush National Historical Park 6, 36, 42, 63, 70-76
Klondike gold rush 4, 12, 13, 15, 16, 28, 70
Klondike Highway 2 6, 36, 44, 45, 63, 69
Klondike Nugget 15
Klondike River 15

78   ALASKA GEOGRAPHIC®

Klondike Trading Co. 67
Knorr, Inez 46

Ladies' Aid Society 55
Lake Bennett 10, 16, 17, 21, 23, 32, 34, 53, 63, 74
Lake Lindeman 12, 13, 17, 62
Larson, Carl 24
Larson, Edith Feero 57
Larson, Stewart 24
Lead contamination 66
Lee, Jack 62
Lewes River, diversion of water 62
Liarsville 53
Lindeman City 74
Log Cabin camp 18
London, Jack 21
Long Bay 2
Longshoreman's strike 27
Lower Dewey Lake 46, 49, 51, 55, 67
Lunde, Pete 34
Lynch and Kennedy Dry Goods 74
Lynden Inc. 64, 67
Lynn Canal 2, 4, 8, 10, 13, 55

MacDonald, Alexander 25
"Madam Jan's Gold Panning Camp" 45, 53
Mahle, Andrew 61
Mallott, Byron 62
Market gardeners 39
Mason, Skookum Jim 12, 15
Matthews, William E. 40
McAllister, Ward 62
McCabe College 45, 50
McCann, Mrs. 57
Merrell, Bruce 2
Mines, Canadian 4, 32, 34-36, 42, 64, 67
Moe, Malcolm 68
"Money King of Alaska" 55
Moore, Bernard 6, 10, 12, 13, 15
Moore, Capt. William 5, 10, 12, 13, 15, 18, 56
Mooresville 6, 8, 10, 15
Morgan, Tom 2
Muir, John 15
Mullen, Suzanne 66
Mulvihill, Carl 2, 64
Mulvihill, W.J. 49
Munn, Henry Toke 25

Nahku Bay 2
National Bank of Alaska 55
"Never Cry Wolf" 53

Newsboys 23
Nicolai, Henry E. 39
93rd Engineer General Service Regiment 44, 59
Norris, Frank 2, 38
North American Trading and Transportation Co. 12
North West Mounted Police 6, 20, 25, 27, 73
Nourse River 18
Ogilvie, William 10, 12
Olympic Hotel 11

Pack animals 18, 20, 23
Pack Train Inn 68
Packers 11, 17, 21, 26, 30
Palm Sunday avalanche 21, 74
Peniel Mission 74
Percival, Dr. Charles G. 55
Phelps, Selby 62
Pleasant Camp 20, 74
Pooley, Charles R.W. 56
Population 4, 53
Portland 8, 15
Portland Exposition 39
Price, John G. 56
Princess Sophia 55
Pullen House Hotel 40, 55, 56, 60
Pullen, Harriet "Ma" 40, 55

Queen 15, 16

Railroad shutdowns 35-37, 42, 64
Rappleye, Su 2
Rapuzzi, Bob 2, 44
Rapuzzi, Charlie 44
Rapuzzi, George 51, 52
Rapuzzi, Rick 44
Rapuzzi, Teresa and Joseph 44
Rasmuson, Edward Anton 55, 70
Rasmuson, Elmer Edwin 55
Rasmuson, Jenny Olson 55
Rasmuson, Maude Evangeline 55
Red Onion Saloon 50, 53
Reed, Morgan 68
Regent Star 66
Reid, Frank 6, 15, 20, 26, 51
Renwick, Pat 55
Reynolds, Mrs. Marian 40
Richards, Jim 52
Richter, Clair 62
Roads 64
Rocky Point 32
Sa Dena Hes–Mount Hundere Mine 67
Sanvik, Doug 53

Satterfield, Archie 8
Schlosser, Agnes 57
Schreier, Rose 2
Schwatka, Frederick 11
Sears & Roebuck 44
Seattle Post-Intelligencer 27
Selmer, Alice Storey 34, 62
Selmer, Betty 60
Selmer, Birdie 34
Selmer, Judy 34
Selmer, Osbourne (Occie) 34
Selmer, Oscar 2, 34, 35, 62
Selmer, Pauline 34, 62
Selmer, Stan 2
Selmer, Victor 34
Selmer, Virginia 34, 62
Sengfelter, Mr. 55
770th Railroad Operating Battalion 33, 59
Sexton, George 38, 39
Shagagwei 13
Shaw, Mrs. E.J. 40
Sheep Camp 20, 74, 76
Shorthill, Mrs. S.E. 55
Sipprell, Guy 25, 27, 49
Sipprell, Walt 62
Sipprell, Winnie 62
Skagway Airlines 33
Skagway Bay 2, 10, 12, 13
Skagway Convention 53
Skagway Garden Club 41
Skagway In Days Primeval 13
Skagway River 6, 10, 12, 13, 31, 39, 42, 64
Skagway Street Car Co. 51, 53, 57
Skagway Traditional Village Council 49
Skagway, District of Alaska, 1884-1912 51
Skagway-Dyea competition 26, 27
Slide Cemetery 21, 74
Slippery Rock 37
Smith's Alaska Guards 17
Smith, Jefferson Randolph "Soapy" 4, 6, 17, 20, 24-26, 31, 51-53, 56
Smith, John U. 15
Smuggler's Cove 13, 51
Snell, Charles 72
Sparks, Abby 57
Sparks, Vic 27, 64
Speer, Mrs. W. Lyle 40
Spude, Robert 50
St. Pius X Mission 61, 62
Steele, Sam 6
Stewart, John 25

Stick Indians 10
Strong, Annie Hall 16
Sun Viking 66

Tagish tribe 10, 12
Taiya Inlet 2, 4, 10, 18, 28, 64
Taiya River 20, 61, 62, 63
Tancred, Sir Thomas 30
Taylor, Marvin 37
Taylor, Paula 37
Temperance movement 55
Tent City tourist attraction 53, 64
Tent restaurants 16
The Committee of 101 25
The Dyea Trail 26, 27
The God of His Fathers, Tales of the Klondike and the Yukon 21
The Islander 15
The Last Grand Adventure 10, 18
The Scales 20, 72, 76
The Skaguay News 16, 23, 24, 27, 32, 38
340th Engineer General Service Regiment 59
348th Longshore Battalion 59
Tlingits 10, 11, 13, 26, 49, 65
Toll Gate War 31
Toll roads 28, 30
Tourism 2, 4, 5, 31, 32, 37, 42, 45, 47, 49-51, 53, 57, 63, 64, 66, 67
Trail of '98 Museum 6, 45, 50
Tramways 20, 32
Transportation 6, 42
Trees 13, 16, 38
Troy, John Weir 70

U.S. Bureau of Reclamation 62
Udall, Stewart L. 72
Ungerform, Mrs. 57
United Keno Hill Mines 34
Upper Dewey Lake 46, 51
Upper Dewey Lake Swim Club 46

Van de Wahl, Mrs. 57

Walker, Charles O. 39, 41, 67
Walker, Harry M. 2, 73
Wallace, George 56
Wann, Clyde 33
Warm Pass road 64
Washington Fruit Store 44
Waterfront (Skagway) 18, 33, 42, 66
Wausuck 13
Weather 49
Webb, John Sydney 21
West Creek Glacier 51

West, Mae 53, 57
White Pass 2, 4, 6, 10, 12, 13, 15, 16, 18, 21, 25, 28, 32, 47, 70, 72, 74
White Pass and Yukon Route Railway 2, 6, 24, 27-37, 39, 42, 44, 49, 55, 60, 63, 64, 66, 67, 70, 74
White Pass City 15, 28, 30, 32, 74
White Pass Transportation 67
White, Elmer "Stroller" 16
White, Thomas 12
Whitehorse Star 47
Wild, A.H. 39
Wildlife 13
Willamette 15
Wilson, Edgar 11, 38
Wilson, Lt. Col. William P. 33
Windfest celebration 67
Woman's Christian Temperance Union 55
Women's Club 55
Woodman, Lyman 2
World War I 59
World War II 6, 41, 57-60
Worley, Boyd 2, 69
Wright, Billy 25, 49

Yakutania Point 13, 51
Yukon River 10, 12, 18, 53, 73
Yukon Southern Airways 23

Zinken, Mrs. 55

Photographers

Alaska State Library 16
Anchorage Museum 8, 11, 15, 17, 18, 21, 30, 50
Canadian Government Office of Tourism 13
Dedman's Photo Shop 2, 33, 37, 42, 47
Doogan, Mrs. James 12, 20, 23, 24, 25, 26, 27, 39, 40, 49, 50, 53, 55, 56, 57, 59, 60, 61, 62, 64
Kalen, Barbara Dedman 47
Kelm, Marian 65
Manewal, Ernest 68, 73
McCutcheon, Steve 38, 45
Nielsen, Nicki 28, 31, 36
Rhode, David 74
University of Washington Libraries 32, 36
Walker, Harry M. 2, 4, 45, 46, 49, 66, 67, 69, 72, 73, 74, 76

ALASKA GEOGRAPHIC® back issues

The North Slope, Vol. 1, No. 1. Charter issue. Out of print.

One Man's Wilderness, Vol. 1, No. 2. Out of print.

Admiralty...Island in Contention, Vol. 1, No. 3. $7.50.

Fisheries of the North Pacific, Vol. 1, No. 4. Out of print.

The Alaska-Yukon Wild Flowers Guide, Vol. 2, No. 1. Out of print.

Richard Harrington's Yukon, Vol. 2, No. 2. Out of print.

Prince William Sound, Vol. 2, No. 3. Out of print.

Yakutat: The Turbulent Crescent, Vol. 2, No. 4. Out of print.

Glacier Bay: Old Ice, New Land, Vol. 3, No. 1. Out of print.

The Land: Eye of the Storm, Vol. 3, No. 2. Out of print.

Richard Harrington's Antarctic, Vol. 3, No. 3. $12.95.

The Silver Years of the Alaska Canned Salmon Industry: An Album of Historical Photos, Vol. 3, No. 4. $17.95.

Alaska's Volcanoes: Northern Link In the Ring of Fire, Vol. 4, No. 1. Out of print.

The Brooks Range, Vol. 4, No. 2. Out of print.

Kodiak: Island of Change, Vol. 4, No. 3. Out of print.

Wilderness Proposals, Vol. 4, No. 4. Out of print.

Cook Inlet Country, Vol. 5, No. 1. Out of print.

Southeast: Alaska's Panhandle, Vol. 5, No. 2. $19.95.

Bristol Bay Basin, Vol. 5, No. 3. Out of print.

Alaska Whales and Whaling, Vol. 5, No. 4. $19.95.

Yukon-Kuskokwim Delta, Vol. 6, No. 1. Out of print.

Aurora Borealis, Vol. 6, No. 2. $14.95.

Alaska's Native People, Vol. 6, No. 3. $24.95.

The Stikine River, Vol. 6, No. 4. $12.95.

Alaska's Great Interior, Vol. 7, No. 1. $17.95.

A Photographic Geography of Alaska, Vol. 7, No. 2. $17.95.

The Aleutians, Vol. 7, No. 3. $19.95.

Klondike Lost: A Decade of Photographs by Kinsey & Kinsey, Vol. 7, No. 4. Out of print.

Wrangell-Saint Elias, Vol. 8, No. 1. $19.95.

Alaska Mammals, Vol. 8, No. 2. $15.95.

The Kotzebue Basin, Vol. 8, No. 3. $15.95.

Alaska National Interest Lands, Vol. 8, No. 4. $17.95.

Alaska's Glaciers, Vol. 9, No. 1. $19.95

Sitka and Its Ocean/Island World, Vol. 9, No. 2. $19.95.

Islands of the Seals: The Pribilofs, Vol. 9, No. 3. $12.95.

Alaska's Oil/Gas & Minerals Industry, Vol. 9, No. 4. $15.95.

Adventure Roads North: The Story of the Alaska Highway and Other Roads in The MILEPOST, Vol. 10, No. 1. $17.95.

Anchorage and the Cook Inlet Basin, Vol. 10, No. 2. $17.95.

Alaska's Salmon Fisheries, Vol. 10, No. 3. $15.95.

Up the Koyukuk, Vol. 10, No. 4. $17.95.

Nome: City of the Golden Beaches, Vol. 11, No. 1. $14.95.

Alaska's Farms and Gardens, Vol. 11, No. 2. $15.95.

Chilkat River Valley, Vol. 11, No. 3. $15.95.

Alaska Steam, Vol. 11, No. 4. $14.95.

Northwest Territories, Vol. 12, No. 1. $17.95.

Alaska's Forest Resources, Vol. 12, No. 2. $16.95.

Alaska Native Arts and Crafts, Vol. 12, No. 3. $17.95.

Our Arctic Year, Vol. 12, No. 4. $15.95.

Where Mountains Meet the Sea: Alaska's Gulf Coast, Vol. 13, No. 1. $17.95.

Backcountry Alaska, Vol. 13, No. 2. $17.95.

British Columbia's Coast, Vol. 13, No. 3. $17.95.

Lake Clark/Lake Iliamna Country, Vol. 13, No. 4. Out of print.

Dogs of the North, Vol. 14, No. 1. $17.95.

South/Southeast Alaska, Vol. 14, No. 2. Out of print.

Alaska's Seward Peninsula, Vol. 14, No. 3. $15.95.

The Upper Yukon Basin, Vol. 14, No. 4. $17.95.

Glacier Bay: Icy Wilderness, Vol. 15, No. 1. $16.95.

Dawson City, Vol. 15, No. 2. $15.95.

Denali, Vol. 15, No. 3. $16.95.

The Kuskokwim River, Vol. 15, No. 4. $17.95.

Katmai Country, Vol. 16, No. 1. $17.95.

North Slope Now, Vol. 16, No. 2. $14.95.

The Tanana Basin, Vol. 16, No. 3. $17.95.

The Copper Trail, Vol. 16, No. 4. $17.95.

The Nushagak Basin, Vol. 17, No. 1. $17.95.

Juneau, Vol. 17, No. 2. $17.95.

The Middle Yukon River, Vol. 17, No. 3. $17.95.

The Lower Yukon River, Vol. 17, No. 4. $17.95.

Alaska's Weather, Vol. 18, No. 1. $17.95.

Alaska's Volcanoes, Vol. 18, No. 2. $17.95.

Admiralty Island: Fortress of the Bears, Vol. 18, No. 3. $17.95.

Unalaska/Dutch Harbor, Vol. 18, No. 4. $17.95.

ALL PRICES SUBJECT TO CHANGE.

Your $39 membership in The Alaska Geographic Society includes four subsequent issues of *ALASKA GEOGRAPHIC*®, the Society's official quarterly. Please add $10 for non-U.S. memberships.

Additional membership information is available upon request. Single copies of the *ALASKA GEOGRAPHIC*® back issues are also available. When ordering, please make payments in U.S. funds and add $2.00 postage/handling per copy book rate; $4.00 per copy for Priority mail. Non-U.S. postage extra. To order back issues send your check or money order and volumes desired to:

The Alaska Geographic Society
P.O. Box 93370
Anchorage, AK 99509

NEXT ISSUE: *Alaska, The Great Land*, Vol. 19, No. 2. Alaska's immensity, variety and beauty are unparalleled, symbols of a unique land filled with eye-catching wildlife and fascinating people. This issue will review Alaska's six regions from the forested islands and mountains of Southeast to the snow-swept plains of the North Slope and the isolated mountaintops of the Aleutians. To members 1992, with index $18.95.

The Newsletter
ALASKA GEOGRAPHIC

Where is the oldest wood in the world? Find out on page 92...

By L.J. Campbell

Editor's note: *Kenelm Philip has been selected one of President George Bush's Thousand Points of Light. He also caught the attention of free-lance writer L.J. Campbell who, before she joined the staff of* ALASKA GEOGRAPHIC®, *prepared the original version of this article for* We Alaskans, *the magazine section of the Sunday* Anchorage Daily News.

The Man Who Chases Butterflies

This Lycaena phlaeas arethusa *was captured at Alder Creek near Fairbanks.* (Courtesy of Kenelm Philip)

Kenelm Philip sometimes carries a shotgun when he goes butterfly collecting. He never knows what he will run into when he chases bugs through Alaska's wilderness.

This afternoon, though, he walks the tundra with only his trusty, faded black net. He is hunting butterflies on Murphy Dome, close to his home in Fairbanks. This is one of Philip's favorite butterfly hangouts. On warm summer days, the dome teems with butterflies.

Philip, 60, has studied, stalked and seized butterflies here every summer for the past 20 years. He has been called crazy and mad by some who have seen him.

"I've heard it," Philip says. "I even had one person say, 'You must be the idiot we saw out racing around and waving his net.'

"I said, 'Yes I'm that idiot'"

Maybe so, but no one in Alaska comes close to knowing butterflies the way Philip does. Let other folks have the king salmon, the bears, the moose, the whales, the eagles. Philip just wants the butterflies. "Nowadays I climb hills because there are bugs on them," he says.

He has fought swarms of hungry blackflies, skirted close encounters with grizzlies, mucked through muskeg and scrambled up 40-degree slopes in arctic regions of three nations to catch these delicate creatures. With 84,000 butterflies in his possession — the second largest collection of arctic butterflies anywhere — Philip is without question Alaska's Butterfly Man.

Today's outing is a warm-up for trips to more far-flung hillsides later this summer. So far this afternoon, he has bagged only two *Colias*, a couple of *Boloria frigga*, an old world swallowtail and a spring azure. A good day sometimes nets 80 butterflies. But it is a bit cool and breezy, and a black cloud is moving in.

Philip trudges across a rocky outcropping, down a hill, around a lingering snowbank and pauses. Before him stretches a rolling field of tussocks. He is looking for yet another butterfly before he calls it a day. He knows it is out there. This is *Erebia fasciata* territory. Not much is known about this rare alpine butterfly, except that it hangs out in sedge grass that forms tussocks.

"Where are you *Erebia fasciata*?" Philip warbles.

Suddenly he yells and bounds catlike from tussock to tussock after a black butterfly slowly fanning itself upwind some 50 feet away. He never pauses, never stumbles, in movement surprisingly swift and graceful for his potato-shaped bulk of 200-plus pounds. He runs in a low plié like a dancer, his legs bent at the knees. He sweeps his net. The mesh closes fast. The *fasciata* is his.

"Now this," he says, "is a beautiful butterfly."

As he has done thousands of

ABOVE: *Kenelm Philip, Alaska's leading authority on polar butterflies, poses at 5,500 feet in the Bolshoy Annachag Range, just west of the Kolyma River in Russia's Far East.* (Courtesy of Kenelm Philip)

LEFT: *Boloria distincta lives in rock slides and is usually found nowhere else than on talus slopes or blockfield. This specimen is engaged in a combination of dorsal basking (picking up solar heat by spreading its wings, which have heat-absorbing black scales along the wing veins), and picking up heat on its ventral side by pressing its wings tightly against sun-warmed rocks on the talus slope.* (Courtesy of Kenelm Philip)

times before, Philip pinches the butterfly's thorax to paralyze its flight muscles, then presents it on his palm. It is a dull black on top, but the wings underneath wear striking whitish bands and a tinge of orange. He studies it a moment more.

He gingerly picks the butterfly up with a pair of long, slender tweezers and drops it into a glassine envelope, which he carefully places in a metal Sucrets box. He slides the box into his hip pocket.

"If he'd seen me coming, he would have turned and gone that way, downwind, at top speed. And I would have lost my chance," he says.

"This is a hard bug to get fresh. It tends to come out and get worn in a couple of days."

But because this colony is nearby, and Philip comes here often, he has several drawers of mint condition, albeit dead, *fasciata*. The ones he does not need for his collection he may trade for other arctic butterflies.

"It's useful to have spare *fasciata*," he says, patting his pocket.

When Kenelm Philip came to Alaska in 1965, practically nothing was known about the state's butterflies. That bugged him. Doing something about it turned into the adventure of his life.

He was a physics professor at the time, teaching at the University of Alaska and working as a radio astronomer for the university's Geophysical Institute at the Chena Valley Radio Facility. Philip specialized in tracking bursts of solar radio noise. But he had butterflies on the brain. After 10 years in Alaska, he quit listening to outer space and turned his focus full time to butterflies.

"I found I'd stumbled into a vacuum," he says, blue eyes glinting intently behind oval wire-rim glasses. "It was an area totally unknown. There was a whole series of fascinating problems involving where our butterflies come from and how did they get here."

Philip decided to find out. Thus began the Alaska Lepidoptera Survey. Today, his collection of arctic butterflies is rivaled in size only by the Canadian National Collection's arctic holdings.

But it is more than a body count of dead bugs. Philip has written an assortment of computer programs to analyze and chart the distribution of each type of butterfly, and this helps him see patterns to their flight and habitats.

An easy undertaking it is not. The Arctic is vast; the butterflies small. Unlike a polar bear, which needs hundreds of square miles to live, a butterfly can exist in an area as small as an acre. Discovering all the species that live in Alaska is like searching for an iceworm in a glacier.

Plus, Philip is only one man with limited time — and even less money. He has no direct funding, and only occasional grants for collecting trips. He depends on contributions of supplies, like butterfly storage cabinets, from the Smithsonian Institution, where he is a research associate. The University of Alaska Museum has kicked in some cabinets, too.

Philip draws a small retirement from the university after 21 years of teaching and research; he retired as a senior research assistant with the university's Institute of Arctic Biology in 1986. His retirement checks, supplemented by the kindness of strangers, are basically all that keep the survey going.

Help comes from the oddest places. Philip once asked the

company that makes the little metal boxes for Sucrets throat lozenges if he could buy some for his bug collection. In reply, the company donated several thousand unmarked boxes, taken off the production line before the logo was stamped on.

Getting to remote sites is another big expense. Helicopter lifts at $400 an hour are far beyond his modest budget. So he hitches helicopter rides with other scientific expeditions.

Then there is the matter of time. Summers in the Arctic are fleeting, with a butterfly season to match. Compared to his colleagues in South America with 12 months to track various butterflies, Philip has a month in the tundra, maybe two in the taiga, to catch what there is to catch.

"The field season here is so short, you have to use every day," he says. "You go from 10 a.m. to 6 p.m. You get back to camp and you're absolutely dead. If you've had a good day, by the time you cook supper, then pack all your bugs away and do your log, it's bedtime. And I don't take Sundays off. If the sun's out, I collect."

Volunteers send him butterflies. Philip gives them a starter set — a killing jar, some envelopes and the butterfly version of the Pocket Fisherman, a collapsible net that fits in a pocket. He figures a little more than a third of his collection has come from some 600 volunteers, most of whom nab a bug here and there. He is always looking for more volunteers.

"If I had what I wanted," he says, "I'd have free helicopter time and a crew of paid people scattered across the state. But no government can afford to spend that kind of money on a small project like this. What I've done at the present time has already filled in a major hole in our knowledge."

Butterflies have intrigued man since earliest civilizations. They are found in ancient Greek mythology as messengers of luck or spirits of the dead. But it is easy for butterflies to get overlooked in Alaska, where a glance in almost any direction reveals far larger, more spectacular flora and fauna. A flit of blue or yellow or orange is easy to miss.

Anyway, Alaskans are too busy slapping mosquitoes. Butterflies, unfortunately, tend to hang out in the same places that mosquitoes do. Unless you are in the room where Philip keeps his collection. Open the drawers in his storage cabinets, and you see a palette of the Arctic.

Arctic butterflies generally are not flashy or large. Many species are dark, better to absorb radiant heat that helps them warm up and remain active in cooler, higher latitudes. They may appear drab from afar. But when in hand, the hair and scales on their wings reveal an elaborate tapestry of textures and markings.

"For some reason," Philip says, pulling open a drawer of yellow and black tiger swallowtails, "people in Alaska call these monarchs. If we were to give them a common name, in Alaska the swallowtail would be called the monarch."

Eighty species of butterflies — excluding real monarchs — are native to Alaska, and they occur almost everywhere except the outer Aleutians. Half of them can be found on the North Slope. Add the butterflies found only in Russia's Far East and arctic Canada, and the number of arctic species soars to an estimated 130.

They have a variety of tricks for surviving harsh conditions.

"Butterflies seem to be almost entirely a bundle of reflexes," Philip

RIGHT: *Described as a "beautiful butterfly" by Alaska's top butterfly man,* Erebia fasciata *is an alpine butterfly whose preferred habitat is sedges that form tussocks.* **(Courtesy of Kenelm Philip)**

BELOW: Papilio glaucus *is the well-known tiger swallowtail, often seen drinking at mud puddles along dirt roads in the Interior. Many people in Alaska and Yukon Territory call this species "monarch," even though the true monarch, a large orange-brown butterfly, is not known to Alaska.* **(Courtesy of Kenelm Philip)**

Eagle Summit outside of Fairbanks provides suitable habitat for this Colias hecla. **(Courtesy of Kenelm Philip)**

says. Some, like the mourning cloak, bury themselves in the snow in the taiga and hibernate the winter away in their winged form. Their bodies are full of glycerol, which acts as antifreeze. On the other hand, the larvae of certain tundra butterflies can freeze in the winter and not suffer damage. Still others stretch their lives over a two-year period, an epochal existence compared to butterflies in warmer climates that pass through their egg-larva-pupa-adult life cycle in a single month.

Philip devotes most of his attention to the tundra. "I like being able to see the bones of the landscape," he says, "and I find the simple concept that butterflies can flourish in such a harsh environment fascinating. Of course, these same butterflies are the ones that in most collections are the rarest" — the ones about which the least is known.

Philip has felt the thrill of finding a new species more than once. He has been involved in the discovery of four butterfly species new to science. He has discovered others new only to Alaska. He has named butterflies — something of a crowning achievement for lepidopterists. His accomplishments in the field have been recognized by the naming of a moth after him: *Grammia philipiana*.

In his abstract about *Grammia philipiana*, entomologist Dr. Douglas C. Ferguson writes, "I am pleased to name this species for Kenelm W. Philip, whose Alaska Lepidoptera Survey provided two of the three known specimens, as well as material of other rare, far-northern species."

Philip has found his bugs in some out-of-the-way places, like Bernard Harbor west of Coronation Gulf in Canada's Northwest Territories. He and a Canadian colleague, Jim Troubridge, hitched a ride there in 1988 with the Canadian Geological Survey.

"That was the oddest habitat I've ever seen," he recalls. They went primarily to track a butterfly, a sulfur, of questionable identity that had been caught there in 1916, the last time entomologists had visited the region. Philip and his partner were also keenly interested in finding a black fritillary called *Bolaria natazhati*. Each of them had run into isolated colonies of *natazhati* in other parts of the Arctic, and they were intrigued by the bug, particularly its affinity for barren slopes. Four specimens had been caught at Bernard Harbor in 1916. On this trip, the pair hoped to find the colony.

They found it on their third day there on a gradually sloping, nearly plant-free beach of blinding white dolomite cobble abutting the arctic ice pack. "It was white to the sea, white to the land," says Philip. "And here were these black butterflies

This specimen of Polygonia satyrus *was taken at Haines in southeastern Alaska.* **(Courtesy of Kenelm Philip)**

flying over the white by the hundreds."

More typically, however, Philip looks for butterflies on hilltops, where the males patrol like sentries, waiting for females to find them for breeding. And he scrambles up steep scree and block slopes to get others. "You wish your uphill leg was a foot shorter than the downhill one," he says. "You get very sore feet."

Chasing butterflies and mounting them is only a small part of butterfly taxonomy. Philip is in the thick of several long-running debates among lepidopterists. When you have people arguing about microscopic characteristics, such things as the color of wing hairs or the number of spines on a male butterfly's sex organ, then taxonomy becomes a baffling combination of art and science.

This Parnassius phoebus *was captured along the Teller Road of the Seward Peninsula.* (Courtesy of Kenelm Philip)

It is a case of lumpers versus splitters, says Philip. Lumpers look at diversity and see only minor variations of the same animal. Splitters see any difference as an excuse to name a separate species. "The problem with the Arctic is that it is such a huge area. People have tended to go in, grab a few bugs, come out and name them without getting any handle on the overall variation of the population, to see if the new names are warranted. Some of the problems simply cannot be solved until the fauna is more widely known, and that's part of the reason behind my survey. In some senses, I'm a lumper. I get more of a feeling of accomplishment if I can take a bunch of diverse data and say, 'But look, it's all the same thing.' It doesn't mean I'm right. It's just how I tend to look at it. To make order out of chaos."

Philip has made four trips since 1978 across the Bering Sea to the Magadan Oblast'. These trips have been a highlight of his career. He thinks the Russian Arctic holds the answer to the mystery of the origin of the Alaska butterfly since the land from Siberia to Canada was once connected.

Philip's butterfly survey spans a large part of this Arctic, a biogeographic province known as Beringia. With the increasing attention to the problem of global warming, Philip's butterfly survey may take on new meaning. "This collection is going to be a priceless resource down the road. It's going to be the only thorough documentation of Alaska butterfly fauna during the period 1970 to 1990, or what have you, before the major climate changes hit. I couldn't even begin to guess what some other researcher 100 years down the road might be able to make of having access to a collection that covers the entire Beringian region."

Nymphalis antiopa *hibernates as an adult. They are therefore the first butterflies seen in spring (usually in April in Fairbanks) and the last seen in the fall.*
(Courtesy of Kenelm Philip)

Environments NOW...

Bering Glacier Retreats

By Bruce F. Molnia

Editor's note: *Author of Alaska's Glaciers, Vol. 9, No. 1, of ALASKA GEOGRAPHIC®, Dr. Bruce F. Molnia is Chief, International Polar Programs, for the U.S. Geological Survey's Office of International Geology.*

Located just north of the Gulf of Alaska between Cape Yakataga and Cape Suckling, Bering Glacier is the largest and longest glacier in North America. For much of this century, Bering Glacier has been retreating. This has resulted in the opening of a large freshwater, ice-marginal lake, Vitus Lake, and in most of the glacier's southern terminus becoming an iceberg-calving margin. Erosion of the beach that separates Vitus Lake from the Gulf of Alaska and the lowering of the lake's level may result in the lake evolving into a saltwater bay or fiord.

The ocean beach in front of Bering Glacier is dynamic and has a documented history of rapid erosion for much of the past half century. Between 1957 and 1976, more than 1,000 feet of beach erosion and shoreline retreat occurred immediately west of the mouth of the Seal River, the stream that drains Vitus Lake into the Gulf of Alaska. The great 1964 earthquake produced about 6.5 feet of vertical uplift along the coastline in front of Bering Glacier. Yet, during the same period, in spite of readily available sediment and coastal uplift, the coastline retreated at an average rate of almost 60 feet per year.

Retreat of Bering Glacier is accompanied by the production of a significant number of large icebergs, some as much as 1,650 feet long. These icebergs are among the largest observed in Alaska. Smaller icebergs, generally less than 60 feet in length, float down the Seal River and enter the Gulf of Alaska. Widening and deepening of the Seal River or the breaching of the beach could result in much larger icebergs reaching the Gulf of Alaska.

This oblique aerial of the terminus region of Bering Glacier shows the width of Vitus Lake. The Seal River is located at the top center of the photograph. (Bruce F. Molnia)

When first mapped in detail, during the first decade of the 20th century, Bering Glacier's terminus reached a position that may have coincided with its maximum position during the Little Ice Age, a period that began several thousand years ago and ended in some areas as recently as the 19th century. By 1938, the date of the earliest aerial photographs of the glacier, retreat of Bering Glacier's southern margin had resulted in the development of a 3.5 mile long by 2 mile wide ice-marginal lake at the southern perimeter of the glacier. Surges of Bering Glacier occurred in 1938 to 1940, 1958 to 1960 and 1965 to 1968, resulting in each instance in parts of the lake being temporarily reoccupied by glacial ice. From 1938 to the present, in spite of the surges, the net result has been the continuing enlargement of Vitus Lake. Since the last surge, Vitus Lake has more than tripled in width, increasing to its present size of about 15 miles long by 5 miles wide.

Bathymetric surveys of Vitus Lake's floor show that the lake has at least four deep basins with water depths of 200 feet, 450 feet, 550 feet and >600 feet. A 1991 seismic reflection survey of the three shallowest basins revealed maximum glacial sediment fill thicknesses of 165 feet, 172 feet and 370 feet respectively. An accumulation of large icebergs blocked access to the fourth basin, preventing seismic reflection measurements and sediment thickness determinations from being made in this westernmost basin. What makes the observed sediment thicknesses in these three basins unusual is that they were measured at locations that emerged from under Bering Glacier's ice a decade ago or less. Hence, average maximum sedimentation rates in Vitus Lake are about 17 feet to 35 feet a year. These rates are among the highest sedimentation rates measured in any temperate glacier environment.

Bering Trough, a deep, sediment-floored, 27-mile-long submarine valley is located in the Gulf of Alaska directly offshore of Bering Glacier. Depths in Vitus Lake, in areas that have recently emerged from beneath Bering Glacier, suggest that the deep lake basins and adjacent channels that underlie the glacier are a continuation of Bering Trough. If so, a major retreat of Bering Glacier could result in the exposure of an approximately 60-mile-long fiord system extending from the edge of the Gulf of Alaska continental shelf into the coastal mountains.

In the past, introduction of glacially derived sediment transported by the Seal River into the Gulf of Alaska was a major factor in the maintenance and partial replenishment of the beach in front of Vitus Lake. The widening of Vitus Lake following the last surge has resulted in a substantial reduction in the volume of this sediment reaching the Seal River, and being transported by the river into the Gulf of Alaska. As Vitus Lake expanded eastwardly, it captured the headwaters and sediment sources of many of the streams that had previously drained Bering Glacier's eastern margin. This resulted in the sediment starvation of much of the Gulf of Alaska beach east of Seal River. Except for the small drainage system of the Kaliakh River, which receives a small amount of meltwater from Bering Glacier's easternmost stagnant margin, all of the sediment and meltwater produced along the glacier's southern margin presently enters Vitus Lake.

Landsat images of Bering Glacier's southern margin region obtained during the early 1970s generally showed a large, dense sediment plume emanating from Seal River and extending many miles into the gulf. When sampled in 1976, the plume carried a heavy sediment load; the plume is less noticeable on images from the early 1980s. Observations made between 1988 and 1991 have confirmed that the Seal River transports virtually no sediment to the gulf.

High tides on the Gulf of Alaska coast commonly reach heights of greater than 10 feet. As Vitus Lake's surface is only about 6.5 feet above sea level, tidal action influences parts of the lake as well as the entire length of the Seal River. This, coupled with continued erosion of the Seal River beach because of sediment starvation, could accelerate the transformation of Vitus Lake into a deep-water marine basin. Salt water entering Vitus Lake may cause fine-grained glacial sediment to form clumps, resulting in the sediment rapidly falling to the bottom of the lake. This may explain the absence of sediment in the Seal River.

Continued erosion of the beach; high intensity, low-recurrence-interval winter storms; or even in the long term, global warming or other global change could promote a rise in sea level, which in turn could accelerate the drastic retreat of Bering Glacier and its transformation into a fully tidewater, iceberg-calving glacier.

Rising about 50 feet above lake level, this iceberg is approximately 165 feet long. Too large to exit Vitus Lake, remnants of this berg produced by melting and fracturing will be able to drift down the Seal River into the Gulf of Alaska. (Bruce F. Molnia)

This low-altitude, oblique aerial shows the mouth of the western arm of Vitus Lake, where the dense accumulation of icebergs prevented scientists from entering into the arm. The entire nearground area emerged from beneath Bering Glacier within the last 20 years. (Bruce F. Molnia)

Canadian Miners Go for the Gold

The Snip Mine camp and airstrip lie in the Iskut River valley about 59 miles east of Wrangell. (Cominco)

By Ralph Eastman

Editor's note: *This article is excerpted from "The Snip Gold Mine" by Ralph Eastman, published in the winter 1990 issue of* Orbit, *Cominco's quarterly magazine.*

It was midafternoon on an overcast late August day in 1965, and the Bronson Creek valley in northwestern British Columbia was still damp from a light drizzle. Three Cominco geologists were descending slowly down one of several natural chutes that winter's snow had carved into the thick alders on the face of Johnny Mountain.

Ted Muraro, who had been mapping and prospecting most of the day on Johnny flats, was above and behind his colleagues Bob Gifford and Jeff Parsons, geologists for Cominco's Bronson Creek project. As Ted descended, facing the mountain slope and gripping the alders to keep from sliding, he noticed a spot of dirty yellow sticking out of the mud. Digging in his toes to support himself, he pulled out a pick from his belt. After wiping away some mud, Ted chipped a sample from the rock and reached for his hand lens. It was gold.

Ted had discovered an outcrop from an orebody that would become, 25 years later, Cominco's newest mine — Snip.

By late fall 1990, a cluster of buildings and a nearly 5,000-foot gravel airstrip were nestled at the foot of Johnny Mountain in a natural crook formed where Bronson Creek flows into the Iskut River. This is the Snip gold operation. A narrow road wends its way from the camp up the west face of Johnny Mountain to the portals to the mine.

"It's an exciting mining project for Cominco," says Dave Johnston, Cominco's Vice President, Mine Operations. "It's the Company's first Canadian underground mine since Polaris started operating and our first new mine in British Columbia since Valley (now Highland Valley Copper)."

Snip is 60 percent owned by Cominco and 40 percent owned by Prime Resources Group Inc. At full production, the mining rate will be 330 tons per day, with annual gold output exceeding 93,000 troy ounces. Reserves total 870,000 tons grading .85 ounces per ton, with minor silver and copper values.

"Although it is in a remote location, we expect to be able to keep operating costs below U.S.$200 per troy ounce because of the high ore grade," Johnston says.

As is so common in the mining industry, it has been a somewhat long haul from discovery to the start of production. Snip has been staked and arisen from the dead so many times during the last 25 years. "The Little Mine That Could" might seem a more appropriate name for the operation.

A hovercraft purchased in Australia travels the Stikine and Iskut rivers to bring supplies to the mine site. The hovercraft will also be used to ferry concentrate from the mine to the coast. (**Cominco**)

Exploration activity at Bronson Creek can be traced back to as early as 1910, and Cominco prospectors staked and prospected claims on Johnny Mountain in 1929 and 1930. Following his find in 1965, Ted Muraro and his two colleagues took more samples from the side of the mountain and staked some ground to cover it. The following year some trenching was done, but claims on the property were allowed to lapse a few years later. During the early 1970s it was restaked, only to be allowed to lapse again. Much of the Johnny Mountain claims were restaked by other parties in the late 1970s, and Cominco lost a bidding war to secure them. But in August 1980, Cominco officials learned that the ground covering Muraro's 1965 gold discovery remained unstaked. Cominco immediately restaked the lower slope of the mountain and did some more trenching and sampling in 1981 and 1982. Although work was proposed for the property in 1983 and 1984, it was passed over. At one point, Snip was even offered to another company during negotiations on a separate deposit, only to be refused. In 1986, an option was taken out on Snip by Delaware Resources Corp. (subsequently bought out by Prime), which began funding exploration work.

In spring 1989, all indications pointed to a year-end startup of operations, but ore reserve uncertainty and delays in obtaining provincial government approval led to a production decision postponement.

"We redrilled the deposit at close spacing for mine planning purposes, and the results confirmed the ore reserves at a higher grade, but reduced tonnages," Johnston says. In early July 1990, Cominco announced formally the development of Snip.

Surrounded by heavily wooded mountains, the 4,137-acre Snip property is located about 60 miles north of Stewart in some of the most intractable terrain in the province. The problem of gaining access to such a remote area has been solved with the use of airplanes and a hovercraft.

Smithers, British Columbia, about 186 miles southeast of Snip, is the main staging base for regular flights carrying people and some supplies for the operation. Because the Snip landing site is the only valley-level airstrip in the area, as many as a dozen flights land and takeoff on busy days.

The hovercraft, purchased from an Australian resort, has been converted into an open-deck, 10-ton freighter and ferries supplies along the Stikine and Iskut rivers from Wrangell, Alaska, about 59 miles to the west. The hovercraft is used to carry concentrate from the mine out to the coast.

"Cominco has a reputation of being able to develop producing mines in some of the remotest regions of the world, and Snip is certainly testament to that ability," Dave Johnston says. "But a lot of credit for the Snips and Red Dogs of this world belong to the exploration people who go out and find these deposits. The hard part is finding an orebody."

Gerry Fudge drills in the Snip Mine with a single-boom electric jumbo. (**Cominco**)

On the Rim®...

Gertrude Svarny, Aleut Sculptor

When Gertrude Svarny tackled her first sculpture 10 years ago, she never imagined it would lead to life as an artist. Particularly since she did not know what she was doing. It started when a whalebone washed ashore on the beach in front of her Unalaska home. She carried the whalebone indoors, admiring its texture, alternately smooth, shiny, porous and dull. What, she wondered, could she do with it? From a kitchen drawer, she grabbed an exacto knife and a small metal scoop intended for making melon balls. She set to work. Before long, she had carved out a pair of Aleut masks.

"I never in my wildest dreams ever thought I would do anything like that. I was truly amazed that they resembled something," she recalls with a hearty laugh. "My friends gave me lots of encouragement. They were just delighted with what I did, and so I decided to pursue it."

Today, Svarny is recognized as one of the finest representational sculptors in Alaska. She draws heavily from her Aleut heritage. She works mostly in soapstone and alabaster, carving finely detailed figures of Aleut men, women and children going about daily and ceremonial life.

"I try to envision myself back in those days, the way we lived, cleaning fish, telling stories," Svarny said

Gertrude Svarny polishes a piece in progress in her Unalaska studio. She carves mostly soapstone and alabaster, but also works in ivory, whalebone and African wonderstone. (L.J. Campbell, staff)

recently. "I research and read everything I can about the Aleuts. Some things are things I remember, like the posture of women, like my mother weaving her baskets."

As for the mechanics of sculpting, Svarny taught herself. She could not afford the luxury of formal training and she has managed nicely without it.

Today her carvings are included in nearly a dozen permanent collections. She exhibits her work in Alaska as well as in the Lower 48. At the Trail of Tears Art Show, sponsored by the Cherokee National Historical Society, her sculptures have consistently won top honors. In recent years, she has learned the art of bentwood; her bentwood Aleut hunting visors, replicas of ones worn by Aleut hunters many years ago, are part of the state-sponsored "Bending Traditions" traveling exhibition.

Her work is so demanded that she is several years behind in completing commissioned pieces. Most take her a month or longer to make.

When Gertrude and her husband, Sam, returned to her family home in Unalaska in 1980, she anticipated quiet days of drinking tea and visiting old friends. Instead, her new career has, at times, kept her working 19 hours a day, seven days a week. Sam, retired once from the Army and once from private business in Seattle, enabled her to pursue sculpting by taking over the meals, bookkeeping and the other details of keeping a family going. Now at 61, with arthritis haunting her hands, Gert no longer keeps such long hours. Carving stone is physically demanding, even with the help of electrically powered drills, chisels, grinding stones and buffing rods that clutter her work bench. Long gone are the exacto knife and melon baller.

"I had some kind of desire in me for a long time, ever since I was a kid, to do something but it was always frustrating," she says. "I tried painting in my younger years and it never grabbed, you know, like this did. This grabbed. It grabbed me and I can't let loose, even if I want to."

Svarny works in a small, well-lit studio behind her home. It is a new, two-room affair with large picture windows facing Unalaska Bay. Sam recently built the studio to replace a drafty lean-to where she worked for years. He equipped the new studio

Sometimes, Svarny puts a political spin on her work. Among fish and animals on her "Endangered Species" totem, she included an anguished Aleut face shown in detail here. The whalebone, ivory and baleen totem is part of the Ounalashka Corp. collection. (Sam Svarny)

Like all her pieces, this "Thlingit Dancer" started out as a big block of rock, which she shaped roughly with a hack saw before switching to a progression of drill and chisels. This statue is made of soapstone with the mask of wood, ivory, leather and walrus whiskers. (Sam Svarny)

with a timed heater that kicks on an hour before she comes out to work. She likes that heater a lot.

On this August morning, Svarny applies automobile paste wax to a nearly finished statue — an Aleut woman, slightly stooped in a walking posture. She rubs the wax-coated soapstone to a gloss with a soft cloth. She will next carve intricate designs on raised borders of the woman's dress. A string of tiny ivory fish with black baleen eyes lays on the workbench, ready to go in the woman's hand. Sometimes Svarny weaves tiny grass baskets or carves wooden masks for her figures to hold.

"When I first started out years ago, sometimes I'd laugh at myself. One time I sat for five days. I didn't know what I was going to do. As time went by, you know I'd be working and thinking, and it took me three years to get out the piece I had building up in my head."

Sometimes as a figure emerges, she finds she is carving the face of a friend. "I don't do it consciously and I try to avoid it," she says. "Like this one time, I said, 'Nick, what are you doing down there. You're not supposed to be there.' When it happens, I change it. I don't think it's fair to do a likeness without that person's permission. I just try to make a composite of Aleut features."

In addition to carving, Svarny is active in the community. She devotes time to the Holy Ascension Church, has served on the tribal council and, for most of the past 10 years, has been on the Ounalashka Corp. board. She has spent six years on the board for the Institute of Alaska Native Arts in Fairbanks, and was on the Board of Regents for the Institute of American Indian Arts in Sante Fe, N. M., where two of her four daughters attended

Gertrude Svarny's soapstone and ivory statue, "She Borrowed His Eagle Cape," is in the permanent collection of the Anchorage Museum of History and Art. "I had this great big stone, and I had it about a year on my porch, never getting a clue of what I wanted to make out of it," she recalls. One day her friend, poet Jerah Chadwick, stopped by with something he had written based on two Aleut stories. Svarny read the first sentence — 'and she borrowed her husband's eagle cape' — and called to husband Sam to put the stone on her bench. "It was a real amazing thing to me," she says. "I didn't even have to draw. Usually I'll make a rough line drawing of what I'm going to do, but I didn't even have to do that. It kinda just flowed and came out. Little things trigger a memory, a thought." (Sam Svarny)

school. One daughter, Wendy, lives at home in Unalaska, developing a reputation as a watercolor artist. Gertrude and Sam, now married 41 years, spend vacations traveling to visit their other daughters and families, which include seven grandchildren.

But despite how busy Svarny finds herself, she always is drawn back to her art. "I get kind of frustrated if I'm not doing it. And if I'm away from it a long time, I just have to get back to it.

"Sometimes I'm working and I get these awful feelings like, 'this is never going to work; why am I doing this?' I might work on it for several days and finally I see it coming out the way I want it to, and I feel relief and joy. And then later on, I feel like I'm seeing a human being, like it's really here."

The Oldest Wood in the World

By Carla Helfferich,
Geophysical Institute,
University of Alaska Fairbanks

On a summer day in 1987, researcher Jane E. Francis was busy with her wood saws on Axel Heiberg Island, high in the Canadian Arctic. The wood she cut was not driftwood destined for the camp fire, though it did burn perfectly well. Instead, the wood was to be saved for laboratories and museums because it was 45 million years old. Dr. Francis is an expert on fossil trees, and she was sampling the remains of ancient forests.

Fossil forests are not particularly rare, even in what are now the extreme cold ends of the Earth. That Canada's Far North once harbored stands of trees has been known at least since 1883, when U.S. Army Sgt. David Brainard, a member of an expedition under Lt. Adolphus Washington Greely, found petrified wood on nearby Ellesmere Island. But petrified wood is no longer truly woody — its cell structure has been penetrated and replaced by dissolved minerals. What remains may have the approximate appearance of wood, down to growth rings and bark scales, but it is stone, usually quartz or calcite. What Jane Francis investigated was something else entirely — true wood that had been mummified, not petrified. She was accustomed to working with wood long since turned to stone or reduced to a carbon smear between layers of sedimentary rock, and she even had quantities of perfectly preserved dry leaves and feathery conifer needles to examine.

The most common tree in these high-latitude fossil forests is the dawn redwood, *Metasequoia*, whose modern relatives grow in the wild only in isolated regions of central China. This species dominated northern forests before the ice of the Pleistocene chilled the planet.

The extraordinary state of preservation of trunks and stumps, leaves and litter came about because of floods and chance. When they lived, the trees formed a mostly swampy forest in a broad plain cut by several rivers. Every so often, the rivers overflowed in a massive flood. The rivers carried heavy sediment loads, the eroded products of a mountain range to the west of the forest site. When the rivers flooded, the sediments they dumped on the plain sealed the forest floor, smothering stumps and fallen logs.

The sediment particles were

This oblique aerial looks east over the dissected lowlands of eastern Axel Heiberg Island. This is one of the areas where the remains of fossil, mummified forests have been found in the Canadian High Arctic. (From the collection of Dr. Martin O. Jeffries, Geophysical Institute, University of Alaska Fairbanks)

Looking at this winter scene of the mountains of some of Canada's High Arctic islands, it is difficult to imagine that millions of years ago swamps and subtropical vegetation thrived on these islands. (Third Eye Photography)

extremely fine, so the cap they formed sealed out both rot-causing bacteria and entry of petrifying mineral solutions. That was good luck for future scientists, but still not quite enough. If sediments build up thick enough for long enough — and 45 million years is plenty long — then increasing temperatures and pressures can turn buried organic matter into coal. Yet even though the process of flooding and forest regrowth was repeated many times during thousands of years, the sediments on the old flood plain only built up to a depth of a few hundred feet. That was enough to compress the wood and squash some delicate bits of forest residue, but not enough to change the organic materials into anything else.

The final element of favorable chance was changed climate. The gradual chilling of the high latitudes killed the forests but preserved their remains. As erosion brought the mummified forest close to the surface, the refrigeration effect of the ice age held decay at bay.

The different forest layers document the slow coming of the cold. A subtropical swamp like the Florida Everglades, complete with bald cypress trees and alligators, was replaced during thousands of years by mixed woods including birch and alder, then by stands of pine, fir and spruce.

Today the only woody plant found on Axel Heiberg Island is the arctic willow. Its sprouts may reach only a few inches high, even in the protection of stumps that once bore trees reaching a hundred feet high.

Alaska's 10 Most Endangered Historic Properties

Readers of ALASKA GEOGRAPHIC®'s issue on Unalaska and Dutch Harbor are well aware of the preservation problems facing the Russian Orthodox church at Unalaska. According to The Alaska Association for Historic Preservation, that church and nine other properties are on the list of the state's 10 most endangered historic properties in 1991. The nine other properties are the Anchorage Fourth Avenue Theater; Arctic Village Episcopal Mission Church; Chapel of St. Nicholas and Holy Assumption Orthodox Church in Kenai; Eagle Historic District; Fairbanks Exploration Co. complex; St. Joseph's Catholic Church in Nome; Sitka's Building 29, a reminder of the days when a thriving commerce in furs supported a bustling economy in the capital of Russian America; the sternwheeler *Nenana*; and the Kennicott Mine complex in the Wrangell Mountains, which also appears on the national list of endangered historic properties.

1991 was the first year AAHP published the list. The organization wants to focus attention on valuable historic properties that are endangered because of neglect, erosion, lack of preservation funds and/or development pressures.

Episcopal missionaries operated out of this log church built in the early 1900s at the Athabaskan settlement of Arctic Village, north of Fort Yukon. The Alaska Association for Historic Preservation lists this mission and nine other buildings, boats or complexes as the most endangered historic properties in the state. (Alaska Association for Historic Preservation)

Rolfe Buzzell, president of the association, points out that loss of these properties would remove vital elements of Alaska's past. For more information about AAHP, please contact them at Old City Hall, 524 W. Fourth Ave., Suite 203, Anchorage, Alaska 99501.

New Denali Park Hotel On Track

Site preparation is scheduled to begin this year on the long-talked-about new hotel for Denali National Park. A $7 million appropriation in the National Park Service's 1992 budget will cover site preparation and building of roads and parking lots for the hotel, and relocation of the post office and other support facilities.

The current hotel, a series of wings attached to a central lobby, was set up in 1972 after fire destroyed the original building constructed in 1938. Until recently, bunks in Pullman train cars augmented sleeping accommodations at the hotel. The new hotel, to be located near the entrance to the park, is designed to have 140 rooms and is scheduled to open in 1995.

This illustration shows the planned 140-room hotel to be built in the next few years to replace the current hotel at Denali National Park. **(National Park Service)**

WESTDAHL ERUPTS

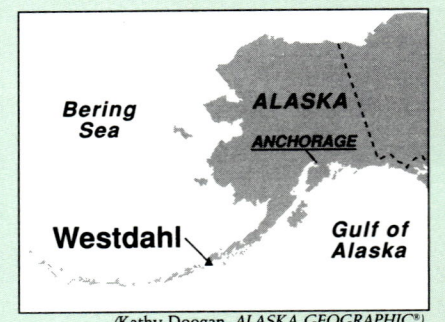

(Kathy Doogan, ALASKA GEOGRAPHIC®)

Alaska's ring of fire flashed once again in November, when Westdahl, a volcano near the southwestern corner of Unimak Island in the Aleutians, sent steam and ash rising more than four miles into the sky. Pilots noted fluid, viscous lava leaking from northeast to southwest trending fissures in the volcano's sides

The Alaska Volcano Observatory reported that the volcano began erupting November 29 after a 13-year hiatus. Westdahl's last officially confirmed eruption was a lava and ash emission in 1978; the following year an eruption was reported in the area that is most likely attributable to Westdahl, but cloud cover prevented scientists from pinpointing its exact source.

Unlike cone-shaped Shishaldin Volcano, 30 to 35 miles to the northeast, Westdahl is a broad, relatively flat volcano, 5,118 feet high. It, and nearby Pogromni Volcano and Faris Peak sit atop a bubble in southwestern Unimak whose topography indicates that the entire area may be a giant, extinct stratovolcano.

Lava and steam escape along a fissure during the most recent eruption of Westdahl Volcano on Unimak Island. **(Sherry Ruberg)**

Northern Ink...

Living Arctic, Hunters of the Canadian North, by Hugh Brody, University of Washington Press, Seattle, 270 pages, 242 black-and-white photographs, five maps, illustrations, bibliography and index, paper, $14.95.

Cultural anthropologist Hugh Brody thinks we can best discover who we are by going to the margins of our world. "Faced with societies and lands that question our everyday assumptions and challenge our preconceptions, it is possible to discover both the importance of others and truths about ourselves," he writes in the book's preface.

To this end, Brody takes us to the vast Canadian Arctic to meet the Inuit, Dene, Cree, Naskapi, Innu and Metis peoples. He focuses on the region's hunters and trappers, their history and their modern lifestyles. Brody's central premise is that these hunters of the north, like most aboriginal and tribal groups, are surviving in spite of stereotypes. He suggests they have long been misunderstood. "Their ways of living and thinking are regarded as primitive, their wealth is characterized as poverty. This denies northern peoples their rights to land, challenges their freedom to hunt, fish and trap in ways of their choosing; it questions parents' responsibilities for their children, and obscures the viability of their ways of life," he writes. "Again and again we must deal with the nature and consequences of these stereotypes."

He does this in 12 chapters with deceptively simple titles such as "Cold," "Meat," "Animals," "Children," "Authority." He also addresses political and jurisdictional disputes

that threaten arctic Natives.

Most illuminating, though, are voices of the people themselves. Some 60 quotations, mostly from Natives with a few from missionaries and early explorers, are sprinkled throughout the book. These statements are presented on pages separate from Brody's text and amount to a running commentary on conditions of arctic Natives by those most affected. The voices include those of Stephen Kakfwi, Fort Good Hope: "When non-Dene came, we saw them as curious strangers who had come to visit; we shared with them and helped them to survive. We could not conceive that they would not see the world as we do. We trusted what people said, for that was the way we had lived amongst ourselves. The Dene had no experience or understanding of a people who would try to control us, or who would say that somehow they owned the land we had always lived on."

And Simon Anaviapik, Pond Inlet: "Our son, the son we loved best of all — we wanted to say no, he isn't going to your school. He was so small, so young. We wanted to refuse. But we said yes. We were intimidated."

And Vince Steen, Tuktoyaktuk: "The people won't take a white man's word at face value any more because you fooled them too many times. You took all the fur, took all the whales, killed all the polar bear with aircraft and everything, and put a quota on top of that, so we can't have polar bear when we feel like it any more. All that we pay for."

The book is illustrated with historical and contemporary photographs, black and white only. The original edition, published by Faber and Faber Ltd., of London, included 17 pages of color plates. In this University of Washington/Douglas and McIntyre reprint, the color photographs were omitted to keep down the price. Unfortunately, the editors forgot to strike a reference in the book's introduction to the color insert, which appeared in the original version.

—*L.J. Campbell*

NEW!

Newsletter INDEX

For those who seek a guide to the wealth of unique information stored in The Alaska Geographic Society's **Newsletter**, we now offer a complete index.

This 10-page index includes an alphabetical listing of all subjects covered in the newsletters for Volumes 15:4 through 18:4. The index also contains a complete listing of photographers who have contributed their colorful pictures to The Alaska Geographic **Newsletter**.

To purchase a copy of the **Newsletter Index**, please send $3.00 to:

**Alaska Geographic Society
Newsletter Index
P.O. Box 93370
Anchorage, AK 99509**

Alaska Place Names, Fourth Edition, by Alan Edward Schorr, The Denali Press, Juneau, 192 pages, no illustrations, index, paper, $25 plus $2.50 shipping.

For years the *Dictionary of Alaska Place Names* has been the standard reference on the state's place names. But several years have passed since the original dictionary was compiled and the United States Board of Geographic Names has continued to make new decisions and revise old ones. *Alaska Place Names*, Fourth Edition, updates readers on decisions made from January 1966 through December 1990. For instance, Mount Adolph Knopf is no longer the name of a 6,015-foot peak in the Coast Mountains northwest of Juneau; it is now known as Mount Ernest Gruening after the former Alaska governor and U.S. Senator. A 7,910-foot mountain east northeast of Mount Michelson in the Romanzof Mountains of the eastern Brooks Range is now designated Mount Deliverance.

A Lighthouse Inspector who sailed Alaskan waters in 1912 and 1913 is commemorated with Hankinson Peninsula, a four-mile-long finger between Dixon Entrance and Torch Bay 47 miles southeast of Mount Fairweather. Cmdr. Ray L. Hankinson (1879 - 1966), of the U.S. Coast Guard was responsible for installation of acetylene lamps as aids to navigation at Alaska's lighthouses.

Some of the entries are not always as complete as an interested reader might like. For example, readers learn that Yang-Webster Peak, a 4,200-foot summit in Tongass National Forest northeast of Excursion Inlet, is named for Yang Shengwu of the People's Republic of China and John Webster of the U.S. Geological Survey, who died in a fall here while doing geologic field work. But the entry does not tell readers when this happened.

Still, in a land notorious for its vastness, a named peak, or river or lake can be somehow reassuring, an indication perhaps that some other human has passed this way before.

All in all, the book clears up some of the confusion from earlier entries in the *Dictionary of Alaska Place Names,* includes the latest geographic designations and is fun reading for serious researchers and casual skimmers.

—*Penny Rennick*

New Map of the Glacier Bay–Juneau Icefield Region

Dee Molenaar, a mountain climber and photographer whose photos appeared in the *Wrangell-Saint Elias* issue of ALASKA GEOGRAPHIC®, has published a detailed map of the Glacier Bay - Juneau Icefield region. Actually, this 24-inch by 36-inch map sheet has several maps, all of which provide information on the state's spectacular Gulf of Alaska coastal areas. The maps' focus, however, is the dazzling glaciers of northern Southeast, particularly the Glacier Bay and Juneau Icefield areas. Drawings of some of the better-known glaciers fringe the bottom of the map. On the reverse is a map of the entire state, another of the Chugach Mountains and Prince William Sound area and a third map of the major glacierized ranges of Alaska and northwestern Canada. The text gives an overview of the state's geologic and ice age history, then moves into a discussion of visits to Alaska's glaciers and glacier studies since 1920.

Order from Molenaar Landform Maps, P.O. Box 62, Burley, Wash. 98322. Cost is $6.50 folded, $8.50 rolled, plus $3 shipping.

PUBLISHED BY
The Alaska Geographic Society

Penny Rennick,
EDITOR

Kathy Doogan,
PRODUCTION DIRECTOR

L.J. Campbell,
STAFF WRITER

Jan Westfall,
MARKETING MANAGER

Kevin Kerns,
CIRCULATION/DATABASE MANAGER

Tracy Reid,
MARKETING/OFFICE ASSISTANT

© 1992 by The Alaska Geographic Society
Box 93370, Anchorage AK 99509